Acclaim for DAN FRANCK'S

SEPARATION

"A story that touches us in our deepest being."
—*Le Monde*

"Unique . . . a sadly exhilarating novel concerned with the gnawing process of moving apart— mentally, emotionally, physically and spiritually."
—*Chicago Tribune*

"Genuinely moving."   —*The New York Times*

"Elegantly written and genuinely felt. . . . [An] emotional story of a sensitive, angst-ridden writer fighting the dissolution of his family."
—*Entertainment Weekly*

"An elegant and emotionally charged sonata on the end of a marriage."   —John Casey

"Franck tells his story with a mixture of shrewdness and humanity. A reader who has patrolled the desert of divorce will recognize the terrain with a pang in the heart."   —Louis Begley, author of
The Man Who Was Late

DAN FRANCK

SEPARATION

Dan Franck is the author of numerous
screenplays and novels, of which *Separation*
is the first to be published in English. Mr.
Franck lives in Paris.

SEPARATION

SEPARATION

A NOVEL BY
DAN FRANCK

Translated from the French
by JON ROTHSCHILD

VINTAGE INTERNATIONAL
Vintage Books
A Division of Random House, Inc.
New York

FIRST VINTAGE INTERNATIONAL EDITION, MARCH 1995

Copyright © 1993 by Alfred A. Knopf, Inc.

The Library of Congress has cataloged the Knopf
edition as follows:
Franck, Dan.
[Separation. English]
Separation: a novel / by Dan Franck
translated from the French
by Jon Rothschild.—1st American ed.
p. cm.
ISBN 0-679-42453-9
1. Fathers and sons—France—Fiction.
2. Marriage—France—Fiction. I. Title.
PQ2666.R2664S4613 1994
843´.914—dc20 93-21795
CIP
Vintage ISBN: 0-679-75444-X

Manufactured in the United States of America
10 9 8 7 6 5 4 3 2 1

For my children

One of the greatest joys in the world, it seems to me, is to be able to share with someone one's ideas, one's feelings, one's impressions. . . . Hmm! This thought is presented in a work translated from German. The title escapes me.

GOGOL, *Diary of a Madman*

SEPARATION

ACT I, SCENE I. A PERFORMANCE OF Shakespeare's *The Tempest*.

They sit on a wooden bench in the middle of the central section of the Bouffes-du-Nord Theater, bent slightly forward at the waist, necks craned in an effort to make out what a mumbling Prospero is saying. In the end they give up, as do their neighbors. Sighs of disappointment from the audience float back to the Duke of Milan on stage.

She sits beside him stiff and distant, wrapped in her black shawl, molten glass earrings dangling. Normally she would lean her head against his shoulder, glance up at his profile, and gently mock his intent concentration. But not tonight.

He takes her hand, a palm lying lifeless in his. Not the merest movement of fingers, nor the barest responsive pressure. Dead skin. He squeezes her fingers and turns to look at her. She stares at the stage, impassive. He takes his hand away and drifts into an austere silence of his own, his mind casting about for plausible reasons for her un-characteristic stolidity. He finds none. Well, he thinks, she'll come around. She never sulks for long.

He listens to Caliban without hearing a word, for the nub of the drama has shifted. He sits straight in his seat, waiting for a hand that never comes. In the second act he capitulates and tries again. She leaves her hand in his, inert but present. He decides to settle for that.

But soon he finds that presence is not enough. He needs the kiss of mobility. He moves his thumb along her fingers and waits. Nothing. He presses. Still nothing. He lets go of her hand and sighs, and she gives it back to him. Smiling, he raises her fingertips to his lips and brushes the skin. She draws her hand away. When he reaches out to take it back, he finds it gone. He puts his palm on her thigh, leaves it there for a decent interval, takes a deep breath, and lets it travel slowly along the length of her leg. She stiffens as it rises, and blocks it with her fist. He takes the fist and holds it, playing with the rings, gauging its resistance, waiting a long moment before slipping his thumb under her curled fingers, caressing the metacarpus with his index and middle fingers. She tenses, and clenches at his thumb, trying to pry her hand free. He holds on, and finally she relaxes, probably because she is afraid the pressure on his thumb might seem like an invitation. He takes advantage of the slackening of her grip to work his fist into her open palm. Forcing fresh contact, he traps her little finger with a creeping motion of his ring finger and gently uncurls her fingers, slipping his between them, folding his fingertips onto the back of her hand and squeezing softly. Their fingers are interlaced now, like lover and beloved in the early days, when you walk through a forest under a translucent spring sky and birds are singing overhead.

"Let me watch the play, will you?" she hisses in exasperation, pulling her hand away and moving it to the opposite side of her body.

On the way out they talk about the production, which neither of them liked very much. But he doesn't give a damn about that. He is waiting for something else, some complaint or reproach, a key that might let him into the closed and lonely space she has thrown up around herself.

They ride home on the motorcycle. She sits wedged behind him, not wrapping her arms around his waist or leaning her cheek against his back the way she usually does.

He asks if she is cold and she says she is. "Put your hands in my pockets," he says. When she doesn't move, he takes her hands—first one, then the other—and thrusts them into his pockets himself. She lets him, but draws back imperceptibly, holding her arms out, palms far from his body. She is a passenger, neither wife nor friend. He has lost the battle of the hands.

HE IS SPENDING MOST OF HIS TIME on the set of a film for which he wrote the story and dialogue. It is a line of work he is not yet comfortable with, and when he comes home at night, he tells her about the problems that have come up. She doesn't listen. She looks at him, but her mind is elsewhere. He wonders whether she is just sick of hearing about it. After all, she had spent most of the summer chauffeuring him back and forth between the country house they had rented and the station, so he could catch the train to Paris, where he was desperately needed to deal with the latest catastrophe.

He decides not to press the issue. The quality of their verbal exchanges has always been a problem between them. He complains that she talks too much, she that he either doesn't talk enough or says the wrong thing, and both admit that they are not great listeners, which doesn't mean that they don't listen.

———

He keeps trying as the days wear on, asking her about the things that usually pique her interest. Sometimes she answers. When she opens up a little, he feels the relief of a man plunging into a warm sea of familiarity after spending too long shivering on shore. The little quirks that have always bothered him still do, but he doesn't show it. He tries hard, looking into her eyes and feeling the waves wash over him. But he is swimming against the current.

She talks, laughs, smiles, comes and goes, does chores. But she shuns him, treating the apartment's narrow hallways like traps to be eluded. She slips rapidly past him, dodging his embraces. Doorways are snares too. Sometimes he lurks there, forcing her to walk straight into him. Then she stands stiff in his arms, elbows flat against her sides, looking off into the distance, without tenderness. It is the same even when they are close, when the connections born of seven years of living together crackle back and forth between them. There are key words he no longer dares speak, automatic gestures he no longer dares perform. Standing no more than a yard apart, they neither touch nor kiss. Little by little, not so much a screen as a void rises up between them, an absence, a new definition of what had been their quotidian complicity.

"What's going on?" he asks.

"Nothing," she replies.

He tries to think of some reason for the distance she is staking out between them, but finds none. They bicker as usual about all the usual things: the division of chores (a housekeeper takes care of everything, except on weekends, when she takes over; he does nothing); how to spend Sundays (he works, she takes the children to the park); the smell of his pipe (which she cannot stand); the ashtrays (which he forgets to empty); the bathroom door (which he never closes); the lights (which she never turns out); the First Child's private school (he wants to move him to public school); trips (she hates driving but has nothing against first-class trains, which he detests); her mania for organization (which he considers a manifestation of anxiety, though he is lazy enough to take full advantage of it); his mother-in-law (with whom he doesn't get along); minor repairs (which he always leaves to the last minute); the TV news (which he always turns off); Sibelius (whom she doesn't care for at all); rock music (too loud for him); his pencils (which she scatters); the telephone (which he uses too much); the bedside light (ditto); the quilt (which she pulls over to her side); the windows (which he closes); the door (which she leaves open); and myriad other issues that any two normal people living together fight about. But none of this can account for any special hostility. In fact, since the birth of the Baby, seven months ago, they have deliberately watered down the conjugal wine, carefully emptying the cup of discord well before it is full.

So he keeps on searching, and keeps on finding nothing. Until finally he comes to a conclusion she does not deny: that he is not the prime cause of the distance.

Sometimes she takes half a step toward him and then immediately draws back, as though afraid to go too far or that he might misunderstand. Each time, he agonizes over the quality of the gesture: was it natural or artificial? Most often he decides it is an instinctive tic or reflex, like the way she sometimes raises her hand to check the catch on an earring she isn't wearing.

He asks her if she loves him and she says she does. He asks the question so often that he begins to feel humiliated. But he cannot help himself. The response is too reassuring.

Then there are times when he tries to boost his

own self-esteem by testing the balance of forces. He strikes a pose, pretending that he isn't much interested either, that he doesn't give a damn about a kiss, a touch, an embrace. He, too, slips past her in the hallway, or plays with the children and walks out when she comes into the room. The trouble is, he is constantly waiting for her to come in, anxiously watching for that shift of the heart that a hand, a mouth, or a look might express. And since he never sees it, he loses the game every time, performing the gesture himself he dreams she might perform but never does. And then, eyes open, she allows herself to be kissed.

He has always lost tests of strength with her.

Only the body language vanishes. The rest still seems solid, the rest being a profound complicity embracing the essential things of life—a like regard born of a rebellious late adolescence, a shared judgment of people, a common devotion to the children's education. This was territory where they had always camped together. They were bound at the roots, even if their leaves often rankled.

She goes about her daily routine, wakes up, takes a shower, gives the Baby his bottle and the First

Child his hot chocolate, gets dressed, settles various material details with him, and leaves for work after offering him her cheek—she is all made up, you see, and a kiss would smear her lipstick. Or so she says. Meanwhile, he stays home, unable to work, spending hours seeking an explanation for the disappearance of signs.

In the morning she spends a long time in front of the bedroom mirror. She is radiant, but without him—or rather, apart from him. And distant, often even with the children.

In the evening, when they visit friends, she drifts away. Her eyes glaze over and she stops talking. She looks more beautiful than ever, but she is dreaming about something else, or maybe someone else. This woman—his woman—whose presence is so powerful, seems to be floating in a strange, mute galaxy. Sometimes, for no real reason, she attacks him as violently as he had attacked her in a past that now fills him with shame. He has no idea what is happening.

From time to time they would meet for lunch. He loved these free and solitary encounters outside home and hearth. Lunch was such a different place from dinner, more autonomous, unconnected to the children that bound them. In the evening they would go out and come home together, but during the day their paths would intersect from separate starting points, and that made him see her differently. No longer the mother of his children and only incidentally his wife, she turned into a new person, one he could seduce, a woman who had invited him to a restaurant where she was a regular. And when they sat down at her table, she would suddenly seem so elusive, her gestures enveloped in the alien mist of her professional life, which he knew of only from what she told him and from these lunches, during which he glimpsed riches that mere words could not convey. Now, however, she denies him these stolen hours. "All my lunches are booked through Christmas," she says.

He asks questions, and gets just one answer: "Seven years together wears you down, you know?" Never more than that. She starts having an occasional whiskey and Perrier at night, something she has never done before. He asks if she is bored, and she says no. If she feels lost, and she says yes. If she is depressed. No. If she is trying to hide something from him. Perhaps. He orbits her endlessly but learns nothing. "Have you met someone?" he asks, and she laughs. "What makes you think that?" Before, she used to say, "How would I find the time?"

She gets up, puts the Baby to bed, and reads a story to the five-year-old First Child. Not so long ago she would call out to him from the children's room, using a pet name. Now she walks into the living room and says, "Okay, you can go in." As though informing the next customer that the toilet is free.

He goes in. Kisses the Baby and plays with him, reads the First Child another story, tickles him, talks to him. In the early days he used to rock him to sleep, making up songs to sing for him, but when the boy turned five they adopted this nightly ritual. He would always be the last to kiss him goodnight, and before going to bed he would slip back into the room, lift the covers, and watch his children as they slept.

When he goes back into the living room, she is taking little sips of her whiskey and Perrier. He sits down. They stopped eating dinner together long ago.

One evening he explodes. They are having dinner with P., a painter friend he has known for fifteen years. A few other people are there too, but he doesn't care. He spends all his time observing and cataloguing the ways his wife's behavior differs from that of ordinary evenings, his mind so totally absorbed in the exercise that he doesn't speak, barely pretends to participate, and doesn't give a damn if he looks like a boor, since in any case that's exactly what he is that night. He is focused on his wife and nothing else, and the attention he pays her is inversely proportional to the extent to which she notices him. At first he tries to respect the social norms as best as he can, since he knows that if he relaxes his self-control for a moment, there will be a scene for sure. He makes herculean efforts to stifle the questions tormenting him: why that glassy-eyed stare; what is that blinking all about; what is she thinking about; would she pull away from my hand, my arm; what's going on; is she ever going to look at me?

She doesn't. And she refuses his arm, his hand, everything. So he provokes her. She responds, and he strikes back, seasoning the spectacle with theatrical flourishes that are mere excuses for avoiding what matters most.

The others follow the performance in uncomplaining and uncomprehending silence. Finally he stands up, grabs his jacket, and says goodbye, falsely debonair. She joins him in the car, and on the way home they continue the scene in camera. At least it stops him from having to take her hand.

He drops her off downstairs and goes back to his friend's place. "That was a bit much," P. says to him when he comes in. He replies that with her there is always a layer on the surface and a deeper layer underneath, one that only he can see (apart from her, of course, since she is always well aware of the reasons for her anger). But he knows this is wrong. That he has always been wrong. The truth is that he is just like her. It is another of the roots that bind them: he could never manage to hide anything either.

The next day no one says a word about it. She is always so magnanimous.

On his birthday she takes him out to dinner at an Italian restaurant. She talks about her work, friends, relatives, the children. The contrast between her idle chatter and the knot that has been choking him since *The Tempest* is insupportable. She spreads varnish in a clumsy attempt to hide an unsightly stain, and he hates every minute of it. He wants to understand, but understand what? She eludes him relentlessly. "Look," he finally says to her, coldly. "Let's stop the minuet. I don't give a shit about your work, your friends, your relatives, or the children. Let's talk about us."

"What do you mean, 'us'? What's there to talk about?"

And then she starts asking questions, far too quickly, about the book he is working on. It is an industrious interrogation, and she listens too carefully to his answers. He knows all her tricks. This is evasive action. He realizes he is not going to shake her, not tonight at least. But now he knows that something serious is up.

THEY GO SEE PAVEL LOUNGUINE'S *Taxi Blues*. He tries the hand game again but loses immediately. It occurs to him that it's hard to live a lie in a movie theater. Habits are habits, and there's not enough space for evasion. It's a yes-or-no sort of place.

It's no.

On the way out she doesn't take his arm. He sinks into another sullen silence. She talks about the film, saying that she recognized the atmosphere he had described the year before, when he came home from working on a documentary in Leningrad. He thinks about the city. He had tried to reach her for ten days and nights, and when he finally got through, she said, "This is the first time we've been out of touch for so long. I wish I could see you."

Those were the days when she gave him her hand, her arm, her lips, her body. *Gentille alouette.* It makes him sad.

He asks if she wants to get something to eat. She says no. He suggests a drink and she agrees. They go to a bar on the rue de Seine and sit on a bench not far from other couples, who are laughing and kissing. They order drinks, and joke about this and that, and after he has covered all the thisses and the thats, he asks again, "What's going on?"

"Nothing," she says.

He presses, but just a little. Later she would claim that he hectored her so mercilessly that in the end she had to give in, but the truth is that the pressure came from her and her alone. All he was doing was searching for the embers of a conflagration fanned by her every smile, her every word, her every absence of words.

Finally she spoke, as if laying down a burden. A trusting smile on her lips, her face glowing with the pride and pleasure of a young girl about to reveal her most secret garden, she said to him, "I've fallen in love with another man."

He looked at her.

"But nothing's actually happened between us," she added.

For the first time in all these weeks he saw real love in her eyes—past tenderness tinged with horror at the suffering she would now inevitably inflict, from this first day to the last.

"You don't love me anymore?" he asked.

"I do," she said. "I do love you."

She took his hand.

They were silent. She was very close to him, but he could not bring himself to caress the palliative palm she offered. First the sword, then the balm. His guts had been slashed, and the hand that had gored him now soaked soothingly in the stream it had opened.

"Who is he?" he asked.

She drew back. Having begun to open up, she now retracted the part of the story that did not concern him. None of his business. Slamming the door in his face. But he knew. He mentioned a name, and she laughed. She was happy. He knew she was happy.

"What are we going to do?" he asked.

"I don't know," she said.

"Do you want me to move out?"

"Certainly not."

"Do you want to?"

"No, we can stay together."

"But if you don't love me anymore . . ."

"I do love you. I do."

"What about him?"

"I love him too."

"And he loves you?"

"Yes, he does."

"I don't believe this!"

He was devastated, lacerated. But he wanted to know more; or rather, he wanted something to hold on to, some piece of handrail along the smooth and treadless staircase he was now sliding down, which she had hurled him down, pushing and pulling with her elegant hands and luminous eyes. My woman, my wife, he screamed to himself as he sat calm and magnanimous, drinking in gulps the fourth whiskey of his pain.

She leaned against him on the motorbike, and later in the bedroom as well. She let him make love to her. She held his hand in hers. He fell asleep immediately but woke up three hours later, as he would now continue to wake up one terrible night after the next, for one, two, three, four months: head on the pillow, opening his eyes to fresh darkness, realizing at once what this dark was made of, a hatchet blow to the nape of the neck, raising his head and lowering it, pulling the covers up so as not to see or hear anything, to sleep, just to sleep.

But he does not sleep. He sits up and looks at her. Looks at her for hours. She is curled up on the far side of the bed, folded into herself, breathing gently. Like a child.

She has not moved by the time he finally falls back to sleep.

When he wakes up that morning, she is getting dressed. Dressing for someone else. Her beauty is dazzling. He gets out of bed and goes into the bathroom.

He wonders what he has done, what he hasn't done, what he should have done, what she expected that he had failed to give. He does not feel the slightest jealousy toward the other man. They are in love with the same woman. Well, she deserves it. The son of a bitch has good taste. We're in the same boat now, you bastard. I could even shake your hand. But since nothing's happened yet, I'd rather you just got lost. I'll fill you in later.

Not that he ever dreamed he was immune to this kind of situation. They had agreed long ago never to tell each other anything. He never had, and neither had she, but she had nothing to tell, as she would later confirm. It all seemed so natural. He could not say she had done anything wrong, and since she had not slept with the other man and still loved him, maybe it was just a fling, an infatuation. After all, they had children. She was the one who had wanted to build something together, and he had let her do it. That meant something. In fact, it meant a lot. They would get past this.

When he comes out of the bathroom and kisses

her, she leans against him, looks up, and murmurs, "Okay?"

"Yeah," he says. "Don't worry."

An hour later he is on his motorcycle heading for the Right Bank, where he has an appointment with a producer he has never met but whom he respects as much for what he hasn't done as for what he has, factors that weigh equally in the scales of quality.

He is on the bridge crossing the Seine when all at once the waters of the river and the waters of his tears collide, and suddenly he is sobbing uncontrollably. He is lost, cast off and abandoned, a tiny image that would become large. He shifts gears and accelerates, and the faster he goes the harder he cries. Self-pity. He is a child, and nothing is more terrible for a child than having to learn to console himself all alone. And he doesn't love himself enough to take himself in his arms.

Red light. People in the cars around him stare. "Assholes!" he mutters.

He angrily lowers the visor of his helmet. "Assholes! Bunch of assholes!"

He speeds down the avenue flat out, in fifth gear. If a cop pulls him over, he will tell him his wife doesn't love him anymore. A good enough excuse for anything, as far as he is concerned. Fuck you all, assholes!

He coasts to a stop in front of the producer's building. His face looks red and swollen in the rearview mirror. He tries to get a grip on himself. Can't go in like this. Okay, wait a while. Be ten minutes late.

As he turns off the ignition, another motorcycle pulls up behind him, just like his, with the man astride whose face he recognizes from a dozen publicity pieces as the producer. He kneels down to avoid being noticed and glances back to see the producer pull his bike onto its kickstand, walk into the building, and disappear into an elevator.

He waits ten minutes, takes the stairs, and rings the bell. The producer opens the door. They shake hands. He catches a glimpse of his face in a mirror and shrugs sheepishly, nodding at his helmet. "Bikes are a bitch in this weather," he says.

Seeing his bloodshot eyes, his host asks softly, "Something wrong with your visor?"

Shit.

They sit side by side in an empty office. There are photographs of a woman and a child on the back wall. He stares at them. The producer is talking, but he isn't listening. At one point he says, "I don't think this project is for me."

"Maybe you should wait until I pitch it to you," the producer answers.

He waits for the pitch. Nothing's happened between us. Yes, I do love you. I don't know what to do. A woman and child on a blank wall. The producer is talking about Europe, drugs, a hellish project, delivery in six months.

He stands up and repeats, "I don't feel like working on something like this."

They promise to see each other again.

Jump cut.

Out on the sidewalk he decides that he cannot let himself go under. He goes to a phone booth, calls his doctor, and makes an appointment.

He explains that he has a personal problem and wants some tranquilizers.

"Have you taken any up to now?"

"No."

"Is the problem serious?"

"Very."

The doctor stares at him affably. He is hoping to hear more, but gets only a sour smile. He writes out a prescription for Valium and Prozac, an anti-depressant. A month's supply, maximum dosage.

"Don't hesitate to come back if this doesn't do the trick."

"Of course."

He runs to the pharmacy and takes the first tablets. On the way to his office it occurs to him that this would be the fourth great sorrow of his life. The first was when his parents got divorced, when he was ten. The second came eight years later, when the girl he had been living with left him while he was in the army in Germany. The third, though quite different, also had to do with abandonment. His deepest miseries were childhood sorrows.

His office is high up under the eaves, in a converted garret he bought with his royalties. He would have preferred a house in the country, but his wife urged him to opt for this room not far from their apartment, a place close to home where he could shut himself in and work in peace.

He had the walls, the floor, the windows doubled, and every day he enters this attic completely sealed off from the outside world. He likes it.

He sits down at his worktable, glances at the last few pages he has written, picks up a pen and puts it down, changes chairs, takes a book off the shelf and puts it back, stares out the window at the Jardin des Plantes, looks at the reflection of his face in the glass, at the photo of his children and the one of their mother. He washes his hands, brushes his teeth, turns on the adagio sostenuto of

Beethoven's "Hammerklavier" sonata, turns it off at the third measure, turns the radio on and turns it off. Finally he lies down on the sofa and closes his eyes. He does not fall asleep. Hours pass.

Late in the afternoon he goes home. He plays with the children, more for their amusement than for his own, since he is only killing time until their mother comes home. He wants her to see him as the irreplaceable Father, down on the floor behind a big pile of blocks, hoping that she will be so moved by the sight that she will say "Hello, my little men" just the way she used to.

When she comes in, he realizes that these are words in a dead language.

Two days later, befuddled by the antidepressants, he goes off Prozac, sticking instead to Valium. A quarter-dose when he wakes up, a second in late morning, a third in the afternoon, a fourth at night.

His sleep is leaden. When he opens his eyes she is already up. He decides to eliminate the last quarter-dose of Valium.

After that he starts waking up at five in the

morning. He lies looking at her and hates these hours because they fly by so quickly. The bed is the only place where he still has her all to himself. He wishes he could make the nights last longer.

He watches the hands race around the dial. When he decides it is safe, either because she has moved or because it will soon be time to get up, he touches her, as if by accident, ass against ass at first and then, even more hypocritically, pretending to be asleep but alert for any sign of resistance. What he is most afraid of is that she will accept only for his sake and not for her own.

But she does not accept. She kisses him furtively, and when he puts his arms around her, she finds excuses to wriggle away. It's too late, or the Baby is crying, or this or that.

He feels no anger or resentment, no jealousy or animosity. He asks no questions about what she is doing. He just knows.

Weekends she wears no makeup and hangs around the house in jeans. Mondays she dresses for work, Tuesdays for the other man. He seems to like black. The leather skirt from Agnès B, the Saint Laurent jacket, big shawls, the imitation-Modigliani brooch. This guy had the same taste as he did. Except that he was the one who had bought all these things for her, and now someone else would enjoy them. As well he should. Yes indeed. Wait till he sees the black silk blouse. And the T-shirt she sleeps in, the one with the New York City seal on the front. And her little-girl slippers.

On Tuesday night he waits fearfully for her return. And kisses her, despite her reluctance.

He is going out to dinner with his best female friend. He mentions it to her, and she says, "I'm going out too."

Normally they would tell each other where they were going, but that day she says only "I'm going out too."

"Who with?" he asks.

An instant's hesitation, and then she says, "With him."

He leaves before her, because he does not want to watch her get dressed and ready for someone else. And comes home early to be the first to go to sleep. He does not want to watch her get undressed and ready for him.

When he gets back from dinner he stuffs himself with Valium in an effort to ward off the temptations of surveillance and deduction. He gets into bed and waits for sleep. Tries to force himself not to think, not to count the minutes.

But he does think, and he never takes his eyes off the clock.

He pulls the quilt up over his face. Takes another Valium and drinks a glass of water. Sinks into a sickening somnolence from which he is roused by every tiny noise from the street or the building. He props himself up on an elbow, hoping to recognize the diesel rumble of a taxi. When he hears one, he waits for the slam of the street door, a step on the staircase, the key in the door. He waits, but it never comes.

They must have had a late dinner, he says to himself. Then he pictures the two of them. Especially her. Okay, if he drove her home, they could be right outside. He pictures her in the car. Or she might be waiting at a station. He pictures her alone on the platform. Or maybe they're kissing. He pictures them. . . .

At two in the morning he gets out of bed in a Valium haze and goes into the kitchen. She comes in at just that moment, and he sees he was right: the other man likes the Saint Laurent jacket and the Modigliani brooch.

"Still awake?" she asks, animated.

He mumbles an indistinct answer and she laughs, tenderly, then comes to him and kisses

him lightly on the lips. He leans into the hollow
of her shoulder, sighs, and closes his eyes. She
moves away.

"You know where we went?"

He shakes his head.

"The Maison du Caviar!"

Caviar. Two weeks ago he himself had taken
her to the Maison du Homard for lobster. She has
taste. And the other man has all the right moves.

They eat out, invite friends over, avoid being
alone together. In the car he asks her to drive so
he won't be tempted to take her hand the way he
used to. And also because he prefers to watch her
watching the road instead of staring blankly at an
indeterminate point off to the right, a point where
hopes alien to him are nurtured.

He refuses to go to plays or movies. Once was
enough. Likewise any of the places they have been
to so often that he would be reminded of the lost
gestures of the past.

Late one night on the way home from a dinner
during which she avoided his gaze all evening, she
grazes a pillar of the garage. "You're destroying
everything I have," he says. "Everything" meaning himself, of course.

He has a stiff whiskey, takes two Valiums, and falls asleep on the edge of the bed, far away from her.

He buys her silk underwear, a pocketbook, earrings, a coat. The coat earns him a kiss on the mouth. A good sign. He proposes that they spend the weekend in Le Touquet.

She agrees.

He begins spinning dreams.

Provided we take the kids.

The dreams veer into nightmare.

He needs his children, but paradoxically he also wishes they were someplace else, far away, because she constantly puts them between them. It's her way of avoiding confrontations, verbal when they appeared inevitable, physical when he holds her just a bit too close. At times like these one of the children always seems to be crying, even if he doesn't hear it.

Well, all right. For the moment, the children are not the problem. It's their mother who is slipping away.

She sits deep in an armchair, whiskey and Perrier in hand. She looks haggard. He comes over to her and asks her what's wrong.

"Nothing."

"Is there anything I can do?"

"No."

An hour later, she has not moved. "We have to talk," he says.

She acquiesces and they go out. Leather armchairs in a luxury hotel in Montparnasse. They order. He wants to be generous. She is hurting, and he wants to help. He hopes that she will always think of him as the person she can rely on most. He is no longer the only one, but at least he can be the most tender, the most understanding. He knows, of course, that tenderness and understanding are mere substitutes for love, but since she does not want his love, he will settle for what he can get. He thinks, naively, that he can be her best friend, her brother, the person whose shoulder she can cry on when things fall apart. Then he will win her back.

He refuses to talk about the other man. A mistake, but he doesn't want to know any more than he already does. He doesn't feel strong enough to deal with the inevitable cruel images. He does not understand, or refuses to understand, that from her point of view the important thing is not so much him, who is right there, as the other man, who isn't. Instead of facing the wave head on, he tries to glide through the trough, asking questions about himself, or about them. He asks whether she wants him to move out, and she says no; whether she prefers to sleep alone, and she shrugs. He sets out comfortably on a path he himself has cleared, but soon gets lost in the thickets when he asks her what she intends to do. "I don't know," she answers.

"Are you going to leave me?"

"Not now."

"Why not?"

"Because I told him I wouldn't leave now."

The "now" hurts less than the thought of the two of them sitting together and talking about him, granting each other sufficient mutual trust to jointly contemplate his destruction, an unavoidable stage in their own construction.

She complains that the situation is embarrassingly petit bourgeois, except that it isn't really a triangle, since nothing has happened. He replies that questions of form are never the real problem. Then he leads her down the only path they still share, the one leading back into the past, toward yesterday and the day before rather than tomorrow and beyond.

She tells him she feels suffocated by the weight of daily life, that she feels he was never there for her, that he paid little attention to her, that he always seemed to be off in his books. All he gets out of that is her use of the past tense. The rest is hardly new to him. He has apologized for it often enough. But she never demanded any apologies. She chose to live with a writer, she says, and she was well aware of how things would be. Deep down she has no real grievances against him. It is just that she has met this other man. Anyway, that's what she says.

For him it is terrifying. You can fight against any reality you can get a handle on, even yourself, but not against outside passions. And that's what he was dealing with here. She loved him, but she was in love with someone else. He could understand that. After all, he was used to characters who regularly kicked over their traces and challenged him, shadows shaped by his own hands only to vanish in painful confusion. But she who had no experience of such unpredictability, while deserving it as much as anyone, was now looking for it elsewhere, for she needed it and always had. He knew that and respected it. Yet he was moved to revolt when he thought of what she said about the weight of daily life. Married couple with two children—it was an image he needed, though at the same time it frightened him. She, on the other hand, was intent on detaching it from the framework of families and turning it into a personal ex-voto. Oh well, he thought bitterly, now is not the time to settle that account. Something more serious was at stake: his children and his wife were like characters getting ready to walk out of his book.

H E WATCHES AS SHE TURNS INTO A different person. The same as before in many ways, but with something missing. Their key words, which constitute their memory, gradually disappear. Soon he will be orphaned from her.

Gestures and tokens of attention fade with the passing days, leaving only ancient traces that rake the wounds. It jolts him when she calls him by a pet name. Two pet names and he dispenses with the day's first Valium. Three would spell happiness. But she no longer counts that high.

She eludes his gaze, as if declining to face their past, even denying that they share a common history. He eagerly awaits the crumbs she might drop him.

He wears the clothes she likes, shaves carefully every morning, and is as attentive as possible. Nothing there.

He walks around naked, lets his beard grow,

and ignores her. Nothing there either. Absolutely no way to reach her.

He starts smoking more and more. Not just his usual pipe, but cigars and cigarettes too. "I can't stand that smell," she says, opening the window.

She never could. Once, two years ago, he had stopped smoking. The first day she didn't notice. Or the second. Or the third. After a week had passed he asked her whether she noticed anything different about him.

"No."

"I quit smoking."

She looked up in surprise. He told himself then that something was wrong between them, that she perceived the negative so much more vividly than the positive. A bad omen, of which he had taken no account. Tobacco is poison.

In the evening he wonders how she will say goodnight.

In the morning he wonders how she will say good morning.

Evening: touch her belly.

Morning: touch her belly.

———

They set out for Le Touquet with the children. He has made reservations in a luxury hotel. On the road she is somewhere else. Hands folded under her pocketbook, pocketbook resting on her lap. A barrier he barely tries to penetrate.

They walk along the beach. It is windy, and kites are flying. Dogs run free, and children wander through the puddles on the sand, past the four-by-fours with telephone antennas. He never cared for seaside walks. He loved the shore, but not the sea.

Images have a power all their own, and since it isn't easy to stroll along together just yards from the waves without holding hands, she lets him take her arm. And there they are—Baby in the stroller, First Child running up ahead—just like all the other families, more or less numerous, spending that Saturday at the beach. Except that they aren't like the others, or only seem to be, for they are thinking at cross purposes, he dreaming up projects she barely heeds.

He thinks to himself: I have her all to myself for two days. Monday she's leaving, and after Monday comes Tuesday.

"We could come here from time to time," he says. "The kids would get some fresh air, you could rest. Rent a place near the beach."

"Maybe," she replies.

He presses on, pointing out the hotels, extolling the weather, admiring the gulls. "I'll teach the kids to fly a kite, and you'll take them swimming in summer." Kites, gulls, swimming—things he had never given a damn about.

He watches her reactions carefully, is soothed by the "Why not?"s and marvels at the "We'll see"s. When she laughs, poking gentle fun at his whimsical plans, he is delighted. For a moment they are accomplices again.

He tries to defend himself: "The thing is, you've poured me into a mold. But I can try to break out of it."

"Sure, honey, sure," she says, laughing. A beautiful laugh.

"What?"

"Why would you do things you can't stand?"

"No, I mean repeat what you said before."

"What did I say?"

"You said 'honey.' You called me honey."

"So I called you honey. So what?"

Seventh heaven. This word, the sound of which he detested not so long ago, now seems suffused with all the charms of this beach, of the kites and the gulls, which he now feels ready to love once and for all. It was true—she had poured him into the mold of his hatreds, which was why he never went shopping with her anymore, why he never went for walks on Sunday, why he lost interest in organizing things. Because every time he showed any desire for this or that, she would say, "Forget it—we both know it's a pain in the ass to you." Thus had she slaughtered all his little desires and petty efforts.

He expresses this thought, not a new one, aloud. "You must be joking," she replies.

But he is not joking. He remembers the first time he had dinner at her place, eight years ago. He had tried to help with the cooking, but she shooed him out of the kitchen. "Plenty of time for that later," she said. Except that later it was too late. He was ready to confess all his sins, but he did grant himself some small absolution.

She had frozen him into a male schema, the very one she fought against in the feminist movement, and he had been delighted to find himself hitched to the masculine totem, since it worked to his advantage. In the meantime, she became a woman, then a married woman, then a married woman with children who called her husband honey and acted just like all her girlfriends, which is to say not like her mother, never like her mother, for maybe a million reasons, just two of which seemed to him essential: this generation doesn't cook and makes love when it feels like it.

All the rest resembled a reproduction stamped out by a slightly flawed press. The shapes were a little fuzzy, but they were there. He recognized some of them—some that applied to her, others to him, others still to the couple they had become, like the merging of two imprints. It was very likely that at thirty-five their parents had taken this same walk in Le Touquet, that they went to Trouville instead of Deauville, to Étretat in the south, or sometimes abroad. If it hadn't been for exceptional circumstances, their life would have resembled their parents', a thought that had often occurred to him when he remembered how he saw his parents when he was ten: as stable people, perhaps a little fanciful, intelligent and free. Whenever he cast about for a way to view himself and his own history, he tried to imagine what his children would think if they were ten. That was the surest measure in his eyes. And most likely they would see him as he had seen his father. Which made him appreciate the ground he had covered. He wasn't seventeen anymore, and neither was she.

He was also able to match their place in the age-and-status pyramid to the things they had done and to the things they had and didn't have. This was a matter of ownership—though less of property and bank accounts than of those little things that seemed so emblematic. When he went into the bathroom, for example, he was always surprised by the number of bottles scattered on the rim of the sink—perfumes, after-shaves, various creams and lotions. He remembered the meager items that made up their kits when they first met, and that told him how much they had changed.

When they went on vacation in times gone by, they traveled light, but now their baggage filled an entire car. Their winter clothes were put away and mothballed in summer, something that astonished him even now, he who possessed a limited but serviceable wardrobe and had long forgotten the childhood lesson that corduroy was never worn after April.

They sent money to the Kurds and to the restaurateurs who donated food to the homeless, gave ten-franc coins to the panhandlers on the rue Mouffetard, and imbued the children, whom they called "the boys," with a multicultural education.

She went to sales at Sonia Rykiel; he owned a pair of Westons. They traveled by air, took taxis, went to openings, and never drank less (and rarely more) than *appellations contrôlées*. They planned their July vacations in February and no longer bought Moroccan sausage sandwiches at demonstrations. They stopped eating cookies at breakfast and drank a variety of different teas. They owned an electric kettle and a Dustbuster, rented a parking spot and a safety-deposit box. They opened the front door of their building by punching in a code, and they gave the concierge Christ-

mas gifts. They had tons of friends who telephoned before dropping in, a pile of work that
kept them busy more than the regulation thirty-
nine hours a week. They had bouts of fatigue and
lassitude and occasional sorrows, but no cause for
grief.

They were grown-ups, and they would often
look at themselves and feel slightly flabbergasted,
as if it had all happened by some pleasant, comfortable, and fairly ponderous magic, like a storm
that never breaks.

All these signs were tokens of their member-
ship in the affluent class to which the radical intel-
lectuals of Paris belonged, marking them for what
they were: modern, independent, middle-class
consumers of the pleasures on offer. Yes, they had
grown up. And since they had grown up together,
it was only natural for each of them to have cast
the other in a role of his own choosing, just as it
was natural for one of them to walk off the set
before the shoot was over, since the roles did not
suit them.

They went back to the hotel in the late afternoon.
She took the children to the pool. He wanted to
go with them, but she said, "Forget it, I know it's
a pain in the ass to you."

He took a quarter of a Valium and poured

himself a whiskey. Then he sat down and began taking notes, and soon a sense of comfort and familiarity, an immense feeling of relief, swept over him, as if he were picking up where he had left off. For the first time in a long while, that feeling of nameless energy returned to him. From his pain he would draw the strength to write, and thereby would recover the only equilibrium now left to him. Nothing else would save him, for writing was the only thing in his life that had never betrayed him—apart from her, if she didn't leave him. If he had created this alien view of his own person, it was because that was the one and only way he could tolerate himself. Writing was his last resort, the sole language left to him.

They had dinner in the hotel restaurant, then put the children to bed and went to have a drink in the bar. They tried to talk about the rain and the beautiful weather, each of them skirting torment. But it didn't last. In her presence or in her absence, he could think of nothing but the situation between them, and he pressed her so hard that in the end she had little choice but to broach the subject despite her reluctance.

She made one last attempt to slip away, appealing to his sense of tragedy. He replied by telling her that things did indeed seem tragic, which she

did not deny, thereby demolishing the frail hope
he had been nurturing. She talked about herself,
for the very first time. Touched, he listened. All
these years he had been waiting for what she was
giving him tonight, deep confidences about what
she was feeling, about the things she resented,
about her hopes and disappointments. For some
reason that remained obscure to him—probably it
was somehow related to this tragedy that she
could not deny—she let herself go, allowing the
concrete walls that had so long protected her to
crumble. He had always respected those armored
battlements, which most likely had enabled her
first to survive and later to live; but he detested
them too, for they concealed the part of herself
that she revealed so parsimoniously that evening,
sipping her vodka cocktail all the while. She
seemed so moving, so beautiful inside and out,
this woman whom he loved and who now perhaps
would leave him. It occurred to him that he might
have gotten himself in this fix by failing to tell her
just how admirable she was, probably because he
didn't think he had to deserve her. And in a way
this new situation was proof of that: if she left
him, it would be, in fact, because he didn't deserve
her.

They got around to the other man. He respected the love this man felt for her, and he told
her so. He would agree to play Jules and Jim, but

probably not for long, though he didn't tell her that. Once again he refused to hear any details about the two of them, shunning the images and pretexts of a jealousy he did not feel. He tried to be noble, and what he was protecting most of all was the road to that nobility. He did not want to end up despising himself.

He sat there looking at her and proudly decided that no one else would ever love her as much as he did. He said so. He also thought that others might show her a less eternal love better than he did. But that he didn't say. A major contradiction between the fundamental and the contingent. He had screwed up the contingent, but the fundamental was still his territory. The fundamental question now, however, was: to what end?

"Are you sorry you told me?" he asked.

She said she was. Because she had been surprised by the force of the blow she had dealt him. And also because, since nothing had happened between her and the other man, she was hurting him with a fantasy that might never be realized. She didn't know it, but that was another blow, raising a question he would now ponder endlessly, knowing full well that its answer would change nothing: Have they slept together? Will they?

"Are you sorry I told you?" she asked in turn.

He said he was. Because now there was no way out and he was condemned to wait.

"For what?"

"For you to make up your mind."

She looked at him, distraught. "Two weeks ago," he added, "you told me you were in love with someone else but that you hadn't slept with him and didn't know what to do. I'm waiting for you to go ahead and do it or break up."

"Break up with who?"

"If you sleep with him, you'll break up with me."

"Why?"

"Because I know you. That's how it'll be."

She finished her drink and they walked back to the room. "It would've been better if you hadn't said anything until you made up your mind. I would rather face a fait accompli than a possibility."

And that was where the tragedy lay, in that narrow margin where every word and gesture is a clue, a clue he could not even interpret, because she couldn't interpret it herself. She waited, and he waited for her to finish waiting.

"I need time," she said after a silence.

"Then take it," he said. "Is there anything I can do?"

"No. None of this depends on you."

"I'm a passive man, a passive man, a passive man," he chanted with a smile.

When they got to the door she turned to him.

"If you ever ask me to move out, I'll leave right away."

He took her by the arm and made her look at him.

"You're waiting for something, aren't you?"

"Yes."

"What?"

"I can't tell you."

A plastic pistol belonging to the First Child lay on the floor near the bed. "Hands up!" he said, holding it to her temple.

She laughed. He took her under the threat of his weapon.

It is like being drowned. She had pushed his head under water, but she is equally adept at letting him up for a quick breath of air and pushing him under again with the merest word or absence of a gesture. From time to time it occurs to him that instead of worrying about trying to swim back to her, he might do better to concentrate on staying afloat.

The small green box of Valium never leaves his pocket, and gets him through the day. The moment he feels torment rising up, he swallows a dose. Little by little the procedure becomes methodical. He reaches for the medicine at times when he knows he is weak: upon waking in the morning, late in the afternoon when darkness gathers. Usually he is as discreet as possible, but sometimes resentment overwhelms him. Then he slices up the tablet right in front of her. "This stuff is really disgusting," he says, leaving her in no doubt as to who is responsible for his dependence on the pills.

They leave Le Touquet on Sunday after lunch, driving silently along a crowded, rainy road, the children playing in the back seat. She stares off to the right, to that vague, alien point. He wonders where she goes during these absences, whether she is thinking of the other man or of him. Of the other man with love, of him with pain. Or of the other man with the pain of love and of him with —with what?

"Don't think so loud," he finally says, unable to stand the silence a moment longer.

She goes into the backseat to give the Baby his bottle, and he adjusts the rearview mirror to observe the scene: mother and children, Daddy driving the family home from the weekend jaunt. Harmonious. Mounting traffic jams, blaring horns, proliferating fishtails, insults hurled back and forth at red lights. The family tableaux seem to fit right in. He hadn't wanted this, at least not this way. But he had done it.

He glances into the back seat again. The boys are sleeping on their mother's lap. A well of warmth rises up within him. "Do you really want to wreck all this?" he asks.

She hesitates, then answers, "No."

"What would you do if we didn't have children?"

"It would be easier."

"What would be easier?"

She is silent.

"Easier to leave?"

No response. He swallows a quarter dose of Valium and examines the situation as coolly as possible. If we were alone, he thinks, it would probably be over already.

He checks to make sure the boys are asleep and says, "We'll never stay together just for the kids." Doesn't even ask her opinion. It is one of those unspoken principles on which they have always agreed, and he knows that her silence means assent.

He readjusts the rearview mirror and heads for Paris. He needs something else now; he needs his friends.

THEY LIKED THE SAME PEOPLE, with whom they shared a like history. They were children of May '68, albeit a few years younger than their elders who had made the smooth transition from the tear gas of the rue Soufflot to the gilded paneling of the Hôtel de Lassay. It didn't take them twenty years to cross the boulevard Saint-Michel, but when they did, it was to take their kids for walks in the Luxembourg Gardens or to eat cakes at Dalloyau's. Without chauffeurs or au pairs.

They had been through Soldiers' Committees, the struggle for abortion rights, the demonstrations against the Larzac military base and the Superphoenix nuclear generator, and various alternative movements. They left home at seventeen, which was a real point of no return, a way of matching their deeds to their ideas, a risk that no one regretted, even if the break with their families had prevented many of them from going on to graduate school.

Afterward they got by on their own.

They were all leftists, but they were never members of the established political groups that leaned rightward on Mondays, Wednesdays, and Fridays and toward the center on Tuesdays, Thursdays, and Saturdays. They were against alternate-side-of-the-street parking.

They voted late and were deeply and viscerally antiracist, antifascist, and antiasshole.

Their friends had moral principles that they stuck to, children they spent a lot of time with, uninvested money, and cleaning women who called them by their first names. They didn't give a damn about racing or the lottery, but they liked traveling; didn't read the comics but liked soccer. They read the papers and went to the movies and the theater, though rarely to mainstream houses. They played few sports, did not collect bonsais, had no life insurance, shunned society dinners, and spent what they earned. Couples saw each other together, but also in pairs, boys with boys and girls with girls. Topics of conversation varied according to the numbers gathered. They talked about politics, culture, work, and children, seldom about food and money, never about cars or computers. They dreamed of what they would do if *this* happened, occasionally complained about the fact that *that* happened. They weren't unhappy with themselves. They yearned for something better but not for more. Everyone knew about everyone else's private life and no one wore kid gloves. They were a little like brothers and sisters. It was a generational thing.

The boys were still macho, less so than in the past but probably as much as they would be tomorrow; the women worked and were free and equal. Both were reasonably faithful and reasonably discreet, generally tender, fairly complicitous, independent of their parents, attached to the memory of their grandparents, and devoted body, soul, and goods to their children.

The girls had a weakness for slightly fashionable haircuts and the boys liked Mont Blancs (the ballpoints, not the fountain pens). They all had Filofaxes. They were the Filofax generation.

"We always thought it would be you," their friends said.

It was true that there had been times in their life together when he had thought about breaking up. Would he have actually done it? He thought not. But he had said it, and first of all to her. More than anything else, it was a threat he brandished to break down her resistance. Never having won any test of strength with her, he would sometimes reach for that crude last resort in an effort to shatter armored walls that he had never been able to scale. He hoped that a collapse would bring them closer. He would take her in his arms to console her, just to console her. But she never let him. Never cried on his shoulder. Nor did she ever simply tell him to cut it out. Instead she would retreat to her bubble and repel him violently whenever he approached. "We each have our cross to bear," she would say. And when, in the heat of a fight, he would sometimes cry, "I can't stand this anymore," she would reply, "Then leave, baby, leave!" with a glint of pride in her eye.

He never left. The most he ever did was to make a show of gathering up his papers, waiting for her to come into the room and ask him to stay. Except that she never came. Or if she did, it was only to ask whether he would be home for dinner.

She never took the threat of a breakup seriously.

The last time he had used it was in Formentera, on a seaside road. "We're going to wind up breaking up," he said. She didn't answer. She was pregnant with the Baby at the time, but he didn't know it yet.

Their friends understood. This was not a generation that held the family sacrosanct. Everyone was
free to stay or leave. A family was a voluntary
grouping that might well be only temporary. Everyone knew that a chance encounter could be
risky, but long-term survival bore an even greater
risk: monotony.

No one was judgmental. "We're here to help,"
they said.

He told his story and listened to others'. Sometimes they were very similar. Often buried pain-
fully in memory, but always ready to rise to the
surface at a moment's notice, barded with blunted
blades that could be suddenly honed by the merest
trifle.

All his friends had been through similar crises,
and this was a generation that did not keep its
problems to itself. In fact, that was one of the
things that kept them from being petit bourgeois,
for the petit bourgeoisie did its cheating in silence.
To them, however, ideas like cheating and being
faithful were beside the point. The words had no
meaning. They didn't understand them. Cheating,
they said, was not a matter of sleeping with someone else. They didn't go in for triangles, or if they
did, everyone knew about it. Yes, someone might

come into your life one day, but instead of turning it into a boulevard play—husband, wife, lover/mistress—in which everything goes on in deep shadow, they played out their scenes in the full light of day. Granted, that might lead to explosion and often did. But afterwards you could pick up the pieces and begin again. You would never forget, but you could start over.

His friends ask questions. He admits that he had not seen the crisis coming. She never expressed any definitive dissatisfaction. In fact, she seemed content with the lives they were leading, as though she had found a balance in it. Then suddenly it all fell apart. He doesn't know if there is a way out, but he's sure they will never be satisfied with half-measures. If in the beginning he thought he could live with the Jules and Jim scenario, it was only because Jules and Jim each knew of the other's existence. He was grateful she had chosen this rather than a Feydeau play.

"Be sure to take your Valium," his friends say.

"Be careful when you cut the doses," they advise.

Or: "Let it melt in your mouth. Take two at

night, never when you wake up in the morning. Have a whiskey without ice with the last one."

They make sarcastic remarks about the tranquilizer confraternity. He is now a full-fledged Knight of the Order of Valium.

He has lunch with S., his wife's best girlfriend, who has known all about it from the beginning. He wanted to see her not to ferret out fresh information but to seek reassurance. He has just one question for her, and she spends two hours dodging it.

"Are we going to get through this?"

"I don't know."

She sits across from him in her T-shirt and denim jacket, looking at him with the tortured expression of a friend who wants to help, but not at any price. Certainly not by trimming or lying.

"But I do have a chance, right?"

"Of course you do."

"How would you rate that chance? Small? Big?"

A regretful pout.

"What should I do?"

"Nothing. You can't do anything. It doesn't depend on you."

She takes his hands and holds them. He can

read the distress in her big, dark eyes. She knows he is hurting and so is she, because the whole thing reminds her of another tale—or two or three—that she herself has been through. He suddenly realizes that he is scaring people. He falls silent.

"Be patient," S. says as they leave the table.

He grasps that piece of advice and charges: "If I'm patient I have a chance?"

"Yes."

"A real chance?"

"Every chance in the world."

She smiles. He thanks her, smiling to himself. He knows perfectly well that he has extorted the answer from her, but he forgets that in no time at all. Yes, he'll be patient. This is war. He's fighting for his life. True, patience is not exactly his strong suit, but he will learn. If he wins, they will rediscover love's madness, in all its myriad declensions. If he loses . . . But he won't.

He takes notes. Not because they might someday be a book, but out of necessity. He is simply unable to concentrate on any other task. Writing makes him feel like he is battening down the hatches, which makes his terrors subside, like the fluttering wings of a bird landing on a beach.

He writes to purge himself, to give some direction to his excavation of his own feelings, and perhaps to win her back. He writes because he cannot do otherwise.

When he rereads his notes, he sees a novelistic dimension in the words and deeds that a hundred thousand others have spoken and lived before him. There are times when all of them—she, the children, himself—seem like characters in a novel that he instigates rather than takes part in. Had he not been a writer, pride would keep him from going on. But a writer at work knows only one kind of pride: writing well.

He keeps his pages in a file folder bearing the label of a regular column he writes for a literary journal: Trash.

He turns down every new job he is offered and postpones those already in the pipeline. "Sorry, no can do," he replies when people lean on him. "My head is on sick leave."

He remembers A.F., one of his female friends, also a writer, who died of cancer several years ago. The last time he went to see her, her hair was cropped short and she was wearing a homespun robe. The walls of her apartment were covered with blown-up photographs of her father, who had died in a concentration camp. She told him that she was battling the cancer just as her father had fought before he died. He understood this need to avoid evasion, to put your finger right on the wound and fight back in exactly that way, naked, despair against despair. That's why he wrote.

He remembered that day well. When she let him in, she showed him an incised lump that had swelled up in her neck. She said her doctor was supposed to telephone to give her the results of the biopsy. The phone rang, she answered, and when she hung up, she said only: "It's a metastasis."

He was now waiting for the next metastasis. Except that whatever happened, he would not die from it. It was the only thing he was certain of.

ER SELF-ASSURANCE, WHICH HE
had never liked, is gone. Her beauty seems
somehow softer, as though a boundless,
hurtful sadness has come upon her. But it suits her
perfectly, accentuating the features he has always
loved most—her frankness and purity, her tenderness and spirit, her incapacity for dissimulation, and also, strangely, a kind of plenitude.

He feels an obsessive physical desire for her.

Their moods seem to move in cycles. When she
is in pain, either for the other man or out of fear
of destroying the seven years of their life together,
he bends over backwards to help her. When she
finally—finally—agrees to let him console her, he
feels both touched and troubled. It never even
occurs to him that the object of her pain might

cause him to lose her, for at these moments they are connected as never before. She is so adorably tender that he forgets. He swears to himself that he will do whatever it takes to remain a *good man*. He is terrified that someday, if she leaves him, he will erect defense mechanisms as odious as all such mechanisms always are. He must never do that. Never.

He drove her to her office. She was wonderfully kind—and totally lost. "If you don't know what to do," he said, playing the grown-up, "I'll decide for you, if that'll help."

She shook her head. "Don't do anything irreparable," she said.

She was afraid. Before she got out of the car she squeezed him tight. There were tears in her eyes.

As she drifts further away from him, he begins to see her in a new light, as a woman no longer his and whom he must now win over and love. It is as though she were becoming an alien part of himself. He sees her as a doe. As his doe.

Sometimes he tells himself that a woman getting ready to leave a man could not be so loving. But he is not sure whether the tenderness she now shows him, unlike anything he had known before, is the product of her love for him, of her anger, of her inability to tolerate the situation any longer, or of her terror. Perhaps she fears that she will lose control, or that he will not, thus running the risk of ruining everything. She is afraid to make any definitive move, and she does not want him to do anything either. She fears the irreparable. A doe caught in the cross hairs.

Pain gripped him.

One day, as he stared at the photograph of her he still kept on his desk, he was swept by a fit of rage. What right did she have to cause him so much pain? He hid the photograph and threw her office phone number away. She looked too beautiful in the photograph, and he did not want to call her, or even think about her. All he wanted was to forget.

One day he had lunch with another woman and thought about taking off his wedding ring. But he didn't. He told himself it would be disloyal. Also that it might be an omen.

———

He soothes his nerves by drinking a little. He smokes too much. Loses weight. Eats only to keep hunger at bay. He doesn't feel like doing anything.

Sometimes she is nice to him because she has seen the other man (generally on Tuesday); sometimes she is cold because she has not seen him, and presumably resents him for being there instead. Then he yearns for some small act of kindness. He angles for it. He feels weighed down.

One morning he woke up in the grip of pain. The next day it overwhelmed him. And so it went, hour by hour, day by day. He struggled up and was cast back down.

He is incapable of any resolution. He tries to be cold and distant, hoping it will draw her back to him, but he cannot resist the need to feel her head against his shoulder for long. She rules him.

———

Each night he records the daily temperature in his notebook, hoping to be able to trace out a curve and thereby discover the locus of his mood swings. He writes: Good, Average, Tough, Horrible.

Tough is clearly the trendsetter, Horrible a far too frequent entry. It comes mostly when they sit in the living room, each in an armchair, she with her whiskey and Perrier, he with his whiskey on the rocks, with no distractions at all, when the children are in bed asleep and there is nothing to watch on the television, which they rarely turn on anyway. Nothing that might let them forget or step back for a moment or take each other's hand and say, "Let's try to help each other."

He waits for the fortieth day. Five years earlier he suffered an ordeal that lasted forty days. The fortieth day falls on the eve of their anniversary, and he is convinced that *something* will happen then. He feels guilty that irrationality is the only weapon he can find with which to repel his grief.

Her gestures afford him the bare minimum of reassurance, but nothing more. Not long ago she would take his arm when they walked together.

Now she strides along parallel to him, hands in the pockets of the coat he bought her. He hates that coat. Because of its pockets. And because it might be the last present he will ever buy for her.

He feels a void on his left side as they walk. He does not know what to do with his arm, his hand, his wrist, his fingers. His whole left side is orphaned. In mourning.

One angry evening he attempted a kamikaze operation. All at once he saw her as an adolescent, a spoiled child indulging the fantasies of another age, acting as though he were her father or her guardian. He was sick of the uncertainty she constantly dangled in his face. I love you and I love the other man, I don't know, I don't know, you put it all together and you shake it all about. He saw no reason why he should have to oblige her every whim, why he should let her inflict this waiting upon him just because she felt she had to wait, why she didn't decide, why she had drawn him into this hesitation waltz of leaning this way and that, this game of vague possibilities that was ultimately so convenient for her, since it had no consequence and cost her nothing, neither the materiality of her life with him nor the immateriality of her dreams about the other man. He told himself that she had strapped him to a rack and was torturing him day and night with a skill that seemed especially bizarre since she was innocent of all perversity. For the first time, he rebelled, trying to get her to grow up, to come down from her private heaven and rejoin him in purgatory, gauging and grasping the consequences of what he called, that night, her caprice.

He joined her in the living room after the children had gone to bed. He sat down opposite her and said, "We have to think about separating."

She tossed down the remains of her whiskey and Perrier and stood up quickly. He followed her into the kitchen.

"We can't go on like this. We have to talk about the children and the house."

She fled to the bathroom. He went after her.

"We have to talk about divorce."

She went back into the living room. He hammered down the nail of their seven years together, sharpening and resharpening the point so as to hurt and frighten her. An image suddenly crossed his mind: one day, after his own parents' divorce, he stuck the point of a compass into his wrist and turned it round and round to hurt and frighten his father. There was no blood, but he still remembered the slight resistance of the flesh and the sound the skin made when it tore, not unlike a thread snapping.

He sketched the icy portrait of the future for

her. Terrified, she dropped to her knees and coiled against him like a child. "I don't want to hear this," she murmured. "I'm too afraid."

A minute later she was on her feet again, newly cold and distant, as though fear of the present had overwhelmed fear of the future, the prospect of the status quo scaring her more than the prospect of a breakup. The sharp snap of thread breaking. A sound that always seems definitive because you sense it can never be fixed.

When he awoke at four in the morning, as he always did, anguish washed over him. He realized that discussions like the one they'd had that night were pointless, something she understood much better than he did: he sought them out, while she fled them. Whenever they talked about *that*, they entered an intense intimacy that collapsed almost immediately. But if they didn't talk about it, they couldn't talk about anything, because nothing else was important.

He saw his female friends often and his male friends seldom, with one exception: R., who lived with S.

Until his marriage, his friendships had been more naturally feminine than masculine. He had always preferred the company of girls to that of boys, a preference that was probably not unrelated to the joys of seduction. But that wasn't the whole story. His time in the army had left him with a horror of all-male environments, which almost always degenerated into crude chatter about sex. That was something he did not need, today even less than in the past.

It was his feminine side that now came to the fore, and it found a more sensitive response from women, who offered him a tenderness and affection he found indispensable. He broke out of the game of couples, with its idiotically immutable rule: you get together in fours or in pairs, girls with girls and boys with boys.

He has lunch with G., another of his wife's friends who is also a friend of his. As he sits across the table from her, it occurs to him that his wife's three best friends are all beautiful, have dark eyes and dark hair, and are Jewish. And I, too, am a dark-eyed Jew with dark hair. Whereas she is a light-eyed blonde, an agnostic Catholic.

He makes no attempt to worm any confidential information out of G. He has no desire to put her on the spot, and he knows more than anyone else anyway: his wife is not at all in control of her own emotions, and simply because of his proximity, he is able to follow her mood swings more closely than anyone else.

The only thing he asks G. is what he should do and what he can hope for. "Don't talk to her," G. says. "Write instead. She loves the writer in you."

G. is a writer too.

So he writes, leaving letters all over the apartment: short notes in detached tones, declarations of love, tender warnings. Every morning he finds his sheets of paper strewn here and there, and he gathers them up, humiliated that it has not even occurred to her to save them.

"What if the cleaning woman finds them?" he says to her one day.

She begins putting some of them away. Others disappear into the trash.

"I like it when you write to me," she often says. And sometimes, exasperated, "You wrote to me again!"

She is more beautiful than ever. He searches her face and her body for the (very rare) imperfections he knows are there, but he can find none.

———

It was a mistake to raise the possibility of separation. Until then, breaking up had been no more than a terrifying aberration, but now it seemed measurable, as he realized when she began playing a new game. "If we separate," she says, "I'll move to the suburbs. Maybe Livry-Gargan."

It turns into a kind of wordplay between them. When you're in Livry-Gargan . . . You'll come and see us in Livry-Gargan . . . Livry-Gargan isn't that far from the Jardin des Plantes by bus, you know. . . .

They even manage to laugh about it.

One night she came home late in a bad mood. She didn't kiss him, was hateful with the First Child, then dropped into an armchair and stared off into space. He was enraged. He would not allow her to bring home conflicts or problems she might encounter outside with the other man. He struck a new pose, as protector of the family. "I don't see why we should have to put up with your crises," he said. "Either stay or go, but if you stay, you have to really be here." Her only reply: "I can't give up the other man." And then: "Since nothing's happened between us, if I left you, it wouldn't be to live with him."

She seemed completely dejected. Meanwhile, he discovered that anger helped, giving him something to lean on. For the first time he expressed his wishes aloud. "I'm not going to move out," he said. "And I'm keeping the children too." And then, clumsily, without ever asking her to choose, he harassed her with questions.

She refused to say a single word.

Before he went to bed he left a note, an ultimatum, in the bathroom: "Either you love me and come and kiss me before you take your shower or else you leave immediately." He added that in the latter case he would deposit enough money in her bank account so she wouldn't have to move to Livry-Gargan.

When she woke up that morning he held her in his arms and hugged her. She got up and went to the bathroom. He heard water running in the shower. Fifteen minutes later she came back. He knew she would. She gave him a very chilly kiss.

Sometimes, observing other couples, he noticed that after years of living together a man and woman become joined by a tenderness not unlike the kind that bonds brothers and sisters at the age of about seventeen, when they face life's vicissitudes together. But they were acting like brothers

and sisters at the age of fourteen—loud and quar-
relsome, she a bitch, he a pain in the ass.

They now share scarcely a word or gesture about
their situation. She flees any mention of it. He has
the impression that she wants to leave things in
limbo, to wait without deciding anything.

But wait for what?

He remembers what she said in Le Touquet,
outside the door to their room: I'm waiting for
something, but I can't tell you what.

What if the thing she was waiting for depended
on the other man?

He remembers this too: I can't give him up.

He pictures them together, sitting at a corner table
in a café. Perhaps he is holding her hand, and she
is telling him about their fights. The other man,
not twisting slowly in the wind the way he is, gets
to play such an enviable role: Mr. Tranquillity and
Intelligence.

He remembers their first few encounters. They
met at a party given by a female friend they had in
common. She wore a simple black dress and glitter-
ing earrings as fiery as her gray eyes. She sparkled.
They stood face to face and talked, drinks in hand.

The second time was at his place. In those days he lived in a studio in the Latin Quarter. She dropped in with a girlfriend while he was having dinner with a bunch of friends. They went dancing at a Montparnasse club where he spent one of the most brilliant nights of his life, drinking and laughing, seldom venturing onto the floor, wretched dancer that he was. But he loved this place, where nothing was forbidden to him and where he had done just about everything.

That night he discovered that she was a terrific rock dancer. He stood in front of her and clownishly moved his hips, spinning her forward and back like a top. They laughed. He made vague declarations of undying love. She poked gentle fun at him.

The third time was after a lunch he had arranged with one of the great loves of his youth, a woman he had hoped to reconquer. They had agreed to meet out on the street in front of the restaurant, and she arrived just as he was saying goodbye to his date. She threw her arms around his neck and held him with infinite tenderness, as though taking possession of him, sending a wordless message to his date: he's mine and mine alone.

The fourth time, he took her to dinner at a restaurant on the place du Panthéon. They talked a lot, and her charm transported him to the feel of a cloud—light, gossamer, and in love.

The fifth time was alone at his place, a beautiful spring night.

Afterward, with unprecedented suddenness, he broke off all his relationships with other women, in particular one whom he loved very much and had been seeing regularly for ten years. This woman had a son, H., and a daughter, C., to whom he had grown very attached and with whom he had kept in touch ever since they met.

A few weeks later they moved in together, and they quickly got married. Because they felt like it, and not for any other reason.

Now, when he thinks about the other man, he sees himself as he was seven years ago, and he remembers how she was then: cheerful, youthful, not yet damaged by the weight of daily life. She was under thirty and they had no children. They were free. Now the other man has replaced him, or would replace him, offering her a feverish passion that he may not have actually felt but whose shores she would rediscover thanks to him. It was hard to blame her for wanting to test the waters.

He knows that he should be her best friend: attentive, amiable, calm. He feels he could do it if only she would acknowledge the danger they face even while insisting on her desire to stay. But he keeps banging his head against the eternal I Don't

Know. And so it is that, imperiled as he is, he senses she will eventually leave him. By now he feels sure of it. But first she has to let the fruit ripen. And there is nothing he can do, because he is not the fruit, and neither, come to that, is the other man. Fruit always falls by itself.

The early days of their life together now seem like a dream. Since then they have been trapped in the mutual definition of the faults and qualities each believes to detect in the other. Each is immobilized by nets woven of the other's regard. As a couple they seem immutable. The fantasies of yesteryear, once tools of seduction, gradually fade or are transformed into a frozen grid in which every feature of their characters has its own abscissa and ordinate. Discovery is gone, and only recognition remains. They can be moved by tenderness, but no longer conquered. And the violence of conquest will always carry the day against tenderness, even if only temporarily. Thus is born the turmoil of passion. Thus do those who love lose out to those who are in love. That they love each other he has no doubt. But are they still in love? They have obviously fallen from the state of grace that the other man is now discovering day by day, while he moves further and further away. They are traveling in opposite directions on the road at whose midpoint stands the tree of the state of being in love.

Little by little, yet with remarkable quickness, she donned the sensible suits of a married woman. He often thought that this had been her real wish from the outset. In fact, she made no secret of it. She wanted a husband and two children, and he was sick of endless alcohol-fueled erotic partying. They leaped into each other's arms not only because they were in love, but also because they were in love with what they might be able to build together: a family. Except that now that they had it, it seemed a heavy burden. And that was his fault alone. He was not a man to work eight hours a day, five days a week, eleven months of the year. He wrote constantly, for himself or for his family. Ever since the birth of the First Child he had felt an anxiety that sometimes bordered on panic: that the tools of his trade—his mind or his body, which amounted to the same thing—would wither. And so he worked, using those tools while he had them, and the time set aside for his work became a kind of refuge into which he locked himself, not without pleasure. Since she never complained about it, he never thought it might really be hurting her. But if he had it to do over again, he wouldn't.

———

He would have liked to suggest that they take a trip together, but he knew this was not the time. So all he said was: "Maybe we should spend two months in the States with the kids next summer." She gave no answer, but she was willing to talk about vacations at Christmas (a month away) and Easter. She was in medium-term mode. Not a patch on long-term, but a lot better than short-term.

He took medium-term breaths.

The First Child has a fight with his mother, and she walks out of the room. In tears, the boy turns to his father and says, "Mommy's going to leave me. How can I make her come back?"

He takes the child in his arms to reassure him, and he realizes that the day she leaves (if she does) will be totally, absolutely, and terribly atrocious. He will have to be strong for the kid.

The Baby is too young to understand. He knows that if they break up, he will not be able to keep him. An eight-month-old baby has to stay with his mother.

But the First Child is different. He needs both of them equally. He will not entertain the possibility of his going away with his mother just because

she is the mother. Where children were concerned, women had asked so much of men and
men had given so much to their children that he
could not imagine going back to the way things
used to be. He could not imagine that she might
act as mothers did in the bad old days, automati-
cally demanding custody of their progeny. She
knew all he had done. She knew how deeply
attached to them he was. She would not destroy
that relationship.

Or so he told himself. So he reassured himself.

He is annoyed with her for walking around naked
in front of him, for getting dressed in front of
him, for being so beautiful in front of him. Yet at
the same time he is glad she doesn't close the
bathroom door when she goes in, that she lets him
watch when she does her exercises, that she does
not completely deprive him of the intimacy she
had offered him for so long.

She phoned him.

He asked her which she would prefer: (a) that
I love you; (b) that I don't love you.

Both, she replied.

I don't know, I don't know, I don't know.
Again and always. For how long?

He was stretched out on the sofa in his office when the telephone rang again. It was V. They hadn't spoken in several weeks. The last time had been to wrap up the final technical details of the publication of the book they had written together.

He had barely spoken two sentences when V. interrupted to ask, "What's wrong? You don't sound good."

He told V. everything. V. suggested they get together immediately at his house in Bordelais. He refused. He said he had to stay and fight, that he could not desert the battlefield.

"Promise me you'll come if you need to."

"I promise."

He was happy. He liked V.

The next day the Baby got sick, and he stayed home with him all day. In the afternoon the fever got worse, and he decided to take him to the doctor. He telephoned his wife to ask her where the address book was. There was a pause before she answered, "In the drawer of my night table."

He opened the drawer, and right there on top, open and unfolded, were two letters, one written by him, the other by the other man. He read it without the slightest hesitation.

He called her back as soon as he got home from the doctor's, and he could tell she knew he had found the letter. Embarrassment could be read in her voice, and in her silences.

"You might want to keep our letters in different places," he suggested.

She laughed, and so did he.

They had dinner at R. and S.'s, their closest friends, the only ones they still saw regularly, since they knew everything and had been there for them, as close as any people can be when two tragedies struck them. So great was the intimacy between the four of them that their fights were always fought with bare knuckles, arguments often turning into tag-team matches, the girls going after the boys or vice versa, depending on the circumstances and the accumulated grievances. These were clashes that usually ended in good humor.

But that night the foils were tipped. Girls in the living room and boys in the kitchen (often it was the other way around), both talking about the same thing: their relationships. "You have to think of yourself," R. told him. "Think of yourself first."

"Myself is us. Thinking about myself means thinking about her."

"She has to make a choice."

"She's not capable of it."

"Then she has to get it out of her system. Don't try to stop her."

"I'm not trying to stop her!" he shouted. "She can do what she wants, but let her do it already!"

He was at the end of his rope. When they went back into the living room there was a sudden silence. For the rest of the night they talked about politics.

She's staying! Otherwise why would she have bought him T-shirts?

The turnaround was not long in coming. The start of the weekend was terrible. Not a word, not a gesture. Appalling tension. He doubled his doses of Valium. They sat in their armchairs as the children played, and from time to time he cast a glance in her direction. He knew she was thinking of the other man, but he noticed that she now looked different when she thought of him. Less blissful than before, when every muscle in her face seemed to smile. Her absences now seemed more reflective. His optimistic conclusion was that the passion was waning; the pessimistic possibility was that she was pondering arrangements.

She went into the bedroom and closed the door. He followed, and found her lying on the bed reading. He rested his head on her belly and asked, "Does it bother you if I do this?"

"Yeah. I'm trying to read."

"Well, don't read then."

"Weekends are the only time when——"

"They're also the only time we're together."

Irritated, he got up. She went back to her book.

"Do you want me to leave?"

She shook her head without looking up from the page, and he left the room wondering, in shame, whether he would pay her back for this pain later, if they stayed together. He thought not, but at least he had raised the question.

They ate dinner alone, sitting face to face, without speaking a word. She drank half a bottle of Bordeaux, he a full one. At nine o'clock she went to bed. He went upstairs to visit their fourth-floor neighbor, who had been living alone since her husband left her. He talked, she listened, they had a few drinks. She tried to reassure him, pointing out that even if they broke up, it didn't mean his life was over. Like so many of their friends, she imagined herself in their situation, reminding him how devastated she had been the year before, when her husband moved out. But she got through it, quickly building a new life for herself. Now she was free, and happy.

With a little help from the alcohol, he managed to picture what life might be like if he was alone. It didn't seem all that scary. He could even see an up side to it. For instance, he could hit on this fourth-floor neighbor. And the fifth-, sixth-, and seventh-floor neighbors as well. He would be young again. He would work less, be light as a snowflake. It sounded pretty good.

He left at two in the morning, kissing his neighbor on the mouth and promising her many marvels to come. When he got back to his apartment, two floors below, the door seemed uncommonly heavy. He fell into bed without even glancing at the other side.

When she woke him the next morning, she told him she felt like she had been sleeping in a wine cellar.

They are invited to a reception given by his publisher to celebrate the publication of the book he wrote with V. The two of them are the guests of honor at a banquet he couldn't have cared less about. He tries to fake it, without much success.

She sits at a table far from his, and from time

to time their eyes meet. She smiles, admirably complicitous. It occurs to him that even if they break up, they might still maintain a relationship based on affection and solidarity. But he doesn't give a damn. What he wants is to sleep with her.

She listens attentively when V. talks about the book. When his turn comes, she looks elsewhere.

He talks to one of his best friends, a woman who had been his mistress long ago, and more recently, to remind himself. "So your wife is threatening to have a little adventure with someone else," she says. "So what?"

He replies that he has always respected the pact she herself had proposed: that they never tell each other anything. Besides which, he would never have endangered their relationship.

"Why not?"

"Because I didn't want to leave my wife."

"You would have if you were in love."

"Which is exactly why I never let myself be in love."

That same evening, in a strange coincidence, she says to him, "I always thought that if we ever broke up, it would be on your initiative. I always knew you might leave, but I also knew you would never abandon me, that I could always rely on you. I've never lost that complete trust in you."

"I wish I could say the same," he says with a grimace.

"When you have children together," she concludes, "you never really leave each other."

She is right about that. You might stop living together or sleeping together, you might call each other once a week and see each other once a month, but you don't leave each other. Like the fingers of a severed hand. Side by side in some invisible space. But only people in the process of separating talk to each other that way. Because when they want to disappear a little but not completely, taking some distance without burning the bridge, moving just far enough away not to lose sight of the opposite bank, that's how they reassure each other. To each his own fears. One wants it all, the other only half. And the only weapon in the arsenal of the one who wants it all is to heighten the fear of the one on her way out. By saying things like I can't take it anymore, I'll never see you again. But that was not a weapon he would use. He had never indulged in blackmail.

———

They are having dinner with friends, and he is talking about the shooting of the film he wrote. The story line and dialogue were so badly mangled that he is considering removing his name from the credits. He mentions that just after he got back from vacation he briefly disrupted a nighttime scene being shot in the place de la Concorde because the lines they had put in the mouth of one of the actors were so idiotic.

His wife is sitting opposite him. She backs him up, telling their friends about all the trips he had to make in July and August in an effort to defend his artistic point of view. "They ruined our vacation," she concludes. "Our" vacation. He begins to wonder whether this game might be winnable after all. He decides to commit more pieces to the struggle.

They leave their friends' house at one in the morning. In the street she takes his arm. "Wait till you see what I've got for you when we get home," he says.

She lets him pull her against him. He is jubilant. In the car he checks to see that he has not misjudged the state of play: as he drives he takes her hand. She lets him.

He parks the car in the garage and heads for the apartment. She walks alongside him, slipping her arm into his. A won game. Now he is sure of it.

He waits impatiently for the babysitter to leave. When she is gone he closes the living room door, sits down, and asks her to sit too. He wastes no time. Pawn to king four: "Back when this all started, you once told me that if I asked you to move out, you'd leave immediately. Now I want you to decide. Either stay or go."

She sits very straight, not looking at him, her face suddenly pale. It is the first time he has called upon her to choose. When she refuses to breathe a word, he backs off, disappointed but unbowed. "I'm not demanding anything. Certainly not that you give up the other man. But I can't live with this uncertainty anymore."

"I understand," she says.

He consolidates his flank. "If you want, move out and get it out of your system. I'll stay here with the children for as long as it takes."

He waits, his eyes riveted to hers. He is ready to wait a century to hear the words "I won't leave."

He thinks he has won. He takes a step back, then moves his center pawn one square forward. "All I'm asking is that you try. Say you'll stay, and let's stop living under the threat that you might leave."

She turns to him. A wicked smile flashes across her face, and he knows that all is lost. "I don't know," she says. "I still don't know. But if you force me to decide, I'll have to leave."

Check.

He tries to regroup. "When?"

"As soon as I can work out something for the children."

And mate.

He is choked with rage. "You want it all your way! You promised you would move out immediately."

"Not under these conditions."

She walks out, slamming the door. He follows her into the hallway, then into the bathroom. It is their first head-to-head battle, unchained and inelegant, and weeks of pent-up energy on both sides are ignited in the violence of the blaze. She is hard, intractable, incredibly spiteful. And so is he: enraged by defeat, his heart broken, furious at all the waiting she has forced him to endure for nothing. The dikes collapse. Strategy is cast to the winds and he lets himself slide down the sinister slope of ancient quarrels. When he hits bottom he finds her standing there, rigid, shut down, and nasty. Exactly what they say matters little. The important thing is how they say it. The devastation lies in the force of the explosion, fueled by all the deterioration, the unforgettable resentment, a use of language in which hatred and contempt sweep aside the accumulated patience of past weeks. He can't take it anymore. She was well aware that he would not hold up for long. Once the bonds that held them in check are severed, they throw themselves into a merciless and undignified battle. It is all very spontaneous, random blows delivered in random order, both of them speaking words whose meanings they're not even aware of in the heat of the firefight, their only concern being to inflict the deepest possible hurt. A blitz devoid of all strategy.

The deflagration lasts less than five minutes, and when it subsides, the glass is starred and spangled, ready to be shattered even more perfectly. But neither of them has the heart to deliver the final blow.

She puts the Baby to sleep in the living room and goes to bed. He drags a mattress into the children's room. The First Child is awake. He asks what is happening. And he, knowing full well that he should not do it, at least not at this hour and in these circumstances, explains that Mom and Dad are not getting along anymore. The child sits up in bed, his hair disheveled. "Does this mean you're gonna get vorced?" he asks.

His father takes him in his arms. "Where did you learn that word?"

"At school."

"No, it doesn't mean we're going to get vorced."

"Yes it does. I know it does."

He lies back down. His father stays with him for a long time, wordlessly stroking his hair until the boy falls asleep, cursing himself for his complete lack of self-control. Cursing himself and her too. It had taken all of five minutes for them to forget they had children. Five minutes of hurling any projectile that came to hand, completely forgetting that their two sons, eight months and five years old, were asleep in the next room. He feels ashamed. Of himself as much as of her.

He leaves the room, goes back to the bedroom, and lies down beside his wife. He does not look at her. He stares at the luminous numbers of the clock face. His anger has passed, and he is already wondering how to go about repairing the glass the next day.

Some time later he hears sobs coming from the children's room. He goes in and finds the First Child lying face down, crying softly into his pillow. He picks him up and they lie down next to each other on the mattress he had brought in for himself. He holds him close and whispers, "Sleep, darling, sleep."

The door opens. It is the mother. She misunderstands. Taking a few steps toward them, misjudging what is happening, she hisses, "Don't play that game with him!"

He gets up and leaves. Five minutes later she has not returned. He goes back to the children's room and there she is. The mother has taken his place on the mattress beside his son. An unbearable tableau. She is the one who has done all this, the one who is about to destroy everything, and she has no right to comfort his boys from the grief she herself is causing them! No right at all!

He grabs her by the arm, hauls her to her feet, and leads her back to the bedroom. "Don't switch roles!" he says.

He spends the night lying beside the First Child. It is not the first time he has done that, but today nothing is as it had been. Today, four weeks after the secret was first uttered aloud, the battle for the children has begun.

H E HADN'T WANTED CHILDREN, BUT she had, and he felt a man had no right to deny the woman he loved a child. So they had the First Child.

Two indelible memories bound him to his older son.

The first was his birth.

For symbolic reasons having to do with the history of the place, they had chosen the Clinique des Lilas, known in the seventies for its far-left leanings, which they shared.

The baby was born prematurely, under difficult conditions. A featherweight. The delivery took so long and the mother was in so much pain that the father feared tragic complications. And then he saw what she did not: the birth team's wild agitation, the way they carried the blue-tinged neonate into a neighboring room, the way they slapped him to start him crying, the urgent telephone calls to get an ambulance.

Two hours later the First Child lay in an incubator in a hospital in the fourteenth arrondissement.

He went to visit every day. When they released her from the clinic, the mother went with him. They brought the baby home a month later. The mother went back to work, and for three months he took care of the infant alone during the day. For the next three years he picked him up at the day-care center every afternoon and kept him beside him, putting the bed near his desk and rocking it with his foot as he worked. He kept a constant eye on the fragile baby. He was always afraid he might be too cold or too warm, hungry or thirsty. The mother shared all his fears save one: she never believed anything serious might befall him. But he did. He could never shake the thought that his son might have died at birth, for he had seen the midwife's panic and the obstetrician's haste, and the urgency with which they had carried him away. For these and other reasons—some objective, some not—an instinctive fear that the child might get sick took root within him and inflected his future behavior: he would be unduly cautious, generally apprehensive, maternal in many ways, and very rarely authoritarian.

Then, one day when the First Child was two, he got a phone call from the day-care center: his son was sick; he had to come and pick him up immediately.

He went. The child had a lump on his forehead. They asked him how he got it and he said he didn't know. With the situation apparently under control, the father went home to call his wife. Just as he came in there was another call from the center. His child was in a coma and they were waiting for the EMS. Coma. That was the word they used. Coma.

He rushed back to the day-care center and there he saw his son, unconscious, eyes rolled back into his head. He dared not touch him. He followed the paramedics into the ambulance, and his teeth chattered all the way from the Jardin des Plantes to the Saint-Vincent-de-Paul Hospital, as the siren wailed and the little two-year-old manchild, dead white, lay there not even knowing that the hand he held and the voice he heard were his father's.

He felt he had lived through these two moments—birth and coma—alone with his son, and nothing and no one could ever speak for him, could ever explain what he felt as he stood before the pale, inert shadow of loss and screamed in the ambulance, Let me die instead of him! No one would ever know better than he just how much the love he felt for this First Child was defined by those two events, why he loved to touch him and to kiss him so much, why he always listened when the boy complained that he didn't feel well, and why, one night, he said to his wife: I'll kill you if you take him from me.

He had been afraid to have a second child. The mother-father-child trio was satisfying in its simple coherence and in the exclusivity of the bond he felt with his son. The idea of a quartet scared him. Three had the same mobility as two, while four meant the full weight of a real family. It would call for discipline and rigor, some kind of system. He had trouble picturing himself in that role. He wasn't ready. He wanted to wait.

He also doubted whether he was yet capable of offering a second child the energy he had devoted to the first. The roots of passion he felt for the First Child were anchored deep in the earth. He saw him both as his own son and as that of his characters (even though as he grew, the child moved farther from the tragic shades depicted in his books), not only because of those two dramatic incidents, but also because of the First Child's habit, when he was very small, of breathing in and out so deeply, as if trying to purge himself of a hopelessness that in all probability did not dwell within him.

He had a special relationship with his first boy, intimate and exclusive. And exclusivity cannot be shared. He knew he would feel just as much love for the second, but he did not know how that love would express itself. Oversimplifying, he told himself he could never love another child as he had loved the first. But "as" referred to the manner, and therefore the form, not to the quality, the essence.

The mother was well aware of all this. But she wanted another child. At whatever cost and no matter what happened. He knew that if he refused, they would separate. He did not want that, so he agreed not to wait any longer.

Once the Baby came, he loved him. Passionately. He watched him grow, watched him move, listened to his stomach rumble, rocked him, made up songs for him. He discovered a language with his younger son and became so attached to him that he dared not imagine ever being separated from him as well. Living with a child, he thought, does not mean seeing him every other weekend and during summer and Christmas vacations. Anger choked him when he realized that she might take the Baby away before he learned to say Daddy. Or worse, that he might call someone else Daddy. That his child might even forget him.

———

On the thirtieth day, mad with uneasiness for his children and himself, he called a psychiatrist friend and told him everything. He felt as though he had been banging his head against a wall, and now he wanted a more flexible surface behind which he could find some peace. He wanted a *scientific* view that would free him of his uncertainties. It was a stupid idea.

The psychiatrist told him nothing he didn't already know. But at least he was a psychiatrist, and his words provided just enough strength to loosen the vise for two or three hours.

"None of the men in her life have ever stood up to her," he said. "That's what she expects of you: that you won't give any ground and that you won't abandon her. She's provoking you. This whole business is a web of provocations. Resist them."

Right. But how?

They now begin talking about a possible separation. They do not broach the question of the children directly, but he thinks about it constantly, and so, no doubt, does she, most likely with just as much pain.

He stops going to his garret, staying home instead to protect his territory, remaining as close as possible to his boys, to *his* boys.

———

He asks her to be tender with him for as long as they stay together, and to call him twice a day, the way she used to.

When she doesn't call, he checks the answering machine in his office, hoping to hear her voice. He knows the situation may drag on, but he also knows that time is his only ally.

He would like to steal a moment with another woman who might comfort him. He even has someone in mind, but he does not call her.

The thing that hurts the most is the way she rejects the touch of his hand on her body. He touches her nevertheless, knowing the reason he is so eager to make love to her is that it is the only way of holding her in his arms and squeezing her tight. He wonders how he will handle it, or if he will be able to handle it, if she spends a night with the other man.

HE SOON FOUND OUT. IT WAS THE thirty-first night after she had first told him. The thirty-first.

They spent that Saturday together, trying without much luck to ease the tension between them. She chided him for not going to his garret. He explained that he felt the need to be at home, surrounded by his family, and that he found it impossible to write a single line.

"You always used to spend weekends in your office," she said.

"Not the whole weekend. Just part."

She argued, and he defended himself. It went on for a long time. "Before was before," he finally said. "Things are different now."

It was like that all day long. In the evening, after the children had been put to bed, they found themselves sitting opposite each other with nothing—or too much—to say. Suddenly she turned thoughtful and sweet. "You ought to go out. It might make you feel better."

He went to see his agent, who lived with a screenwriter. Both were friends.

They spent part of the night playing with the couple's child, who had the same first name as the Baby. He felt a pang of anguish as he watched the boy run back and forth between his father and his mother. This sadness, new to him, would now sweep over him whenever he witnessed any such scenes—cocooning, a family together, a child and its mother. But he would have to get used to it.

They talked about what he might do, and the watchword was still the same: patience. Then they spent a solid, whiskey-lubricated hour discoursing on what his best move would be when he got home, whether he should sleep in his own or the children's bedroom. He said he felt like the children's. "Then sleep in their room," his friends advised.

The moment he came in, he realized the question was moot. She wasn't there. The young girl babysitting the children was asleep on the living room couch. The bedroom was empty. It was one o'clock in the morning.

He woke the babysitter, paid her, took half a Valium, and went to bed. At four in the morning the Baby started to cry. He gave him a bottle. It was very unusual for the child to wake up at that hour, and he thought to himself: It's now.

He went back to bed. There was no need to wonder, because he knew. He tried to convince himself that it would change nothing in the situation, except perhaps to clarify it, that they might at last break out of the stagnant swamp of uncertainty. In an unfeigned flash of recognition of justice he told himself that he had done the same thing and that it might be no more significant to her than it had been to him. Which was a mistake, as he well knew. At five o'clock she had still not come home. Nor at six.

She's trying to tell me something, he said to himself. She wants to force me to look reality in the face. If she spares me nothing, it is only to make me understand how very important this is. It is as though she does not want to leave the slightest room for doubt, or the tiniest area of peace.

By six in the morning he was no longer concerned about them, only about her. It was unlike her to inflict so much hurt, with such great force. It was unlike her not to be there when the children woke up. She's had an accident, he thought. The car is lying in the road somewhere, crushed flat. She's been taken to the hospital, and that's why she hasn't called.

He was mad with worry. It no longer mattered

that she had spent the night with another man. All
he could think of was how deeply he would hate
this man if anything had happened to his wife. He
would damn him forever, in his own name and in
his children's. The pain we would feel would be
so unlike, he thought. In death's presence, the
other man would bear the weight of his adventure,
I the weight of our memories.

He decided to wait another hour and then start
calling hospitals. He tried to shore up his morale
by reminding himself that his books always dealt
with death, that lateness was a wound and absence
a bereavement, that in tragic circumstances he
always looked down at his life line, which pre-
dicted death at thirty, and here he was still alive.
He reminded himself that he had never been able
to back away from this chasm, and that she had
always made fun of him for it: "Lighten up! You
always make everything into a big tragedy!"

The hour passed. Still no sign of her. He went
to the window and stared out at the cars. The city
was gray and drizzly. She was not coming back.
He went to the children's room and then went
back to bed, deciding that eight o'clock would be
the final deadline.

She came in at a few seconds to eight. When he
heard her steps in the hallway, he called out, "I'm
not asleep."

She came into the bedroom, wearing jeans and

no makeup. He looked into her face and saw an immense tranquillity and a fluttering of the eyelids that he recognized immediately, for it betrayed the same spark of joy he had seen that first day, when she'd told him.

She sat down on the edge of the bed, leaned against him, and took him in her arms to kiss him —exactly as she had done thirty-one days before. And he let himself go, put his arms around her, she hadn't had an accident, and the more she let herself relax the more he realized that she looked just like he did when he came home to her after someone else, loving her even more, for always.

He was too close to her, too close to the situation, too much an actor and not a director, to recall his own words: One night with the other man means the end of us.

Even if he had remembered, he would have said, I was wrong.

He did not ask where she had been. All he said was: "Next time call. I was worried."

When she did not reply, he added, "You're crazy to leave me hanging all night without a word."

At which point she stood up and said, without so much as a look at him, "You're right, I am crazy. Crazy in love with this man."

She walked out and went into the children's room.

"You took *my* car to go out fucking!" he screamed.

He found nothing else to say, but any other words would have been equally stupid. He might as well have complained that she had worn clothes he had bought her, that she hadn't taken off her rings, that she had left from *their* place. The simple truth was that he couldn't stand the thought that she had taken a part of himself with her. He couldn't stand the thought that she had kissed him afterward, that she had come back, that she had expressed the same uncertainty, I love the other man but I love you too, I'm crazy in love but I come home. He couldn't stand the thought that she had done it. He couldn't stand knowing. She had broken their pact.

He got up and went into the bathroom. She joined him. She seemed suddenly to realize how distraught he was. Once again she put her arms around him. And then she spoke these unbelievably violent words: "You shouldn't be so sad. I'm still *here.*"

She comforted him, like a child.

He took a shower and got dressed. When he came out she was on the bed, playing with the children. She looked at him, waiting for a reaction. Later she would tell him that she had feared an outburst of rage. But it didn't happen that way. When he saw his wife and his two boys, so perfect together, accomplices on the bed from which he was now absent, he shouted, "What a waste!"

The image of that waste was unbearable to him.

He picked up a bag and shoved the manuscript of the novel he was working on into it. He came over to his children and kissed them. Just kissed them. She walked with him to the door.

"Where are you going?"

"I'm leaving."

She did not try to stop him. Looking straight into her eyes, he added, "Thanks for everything."

He went down the stairs two at a time, trying to move fast enough to stop himself from turning back. He wanted his gesture to be definitive.

In the street he did not turn around. He thought of his father, who had broken up with his mother in exactly similar circumstances. His father, whose path he had crossed in the hallway of the house they lived in twenty-eight years ago, in a southern suburb. The father was carrying a suitcase, and the child asked, "Daddy, where are you going?"

"Far away," his father answered.

"When are you coming back?"

"Maybe never."

That was why he had taken no suitcase, why he had only kissed his boys lightly on the cheek: so that they would not remember the moment when their father left home. And if he rushed quickly enough toward the lot where his motorcycle was parked, it was so he wouldn't turn to see them at the window, so that he, too, would not be devoured by that vision of his children, spinning endlessly like a sob in his memory.

FOR A COUPLE OF DAYS HE WENT from place to place, sleeping at his friends' and making ample use of his best friend of all: Valium. But everywhere he went felt wrong. At night because he could not kiss his children, in the morning because he could not kiss his wife, and all day long because he wandered aimlessly, unable to decide where to go. Everything he saw in the streets, in the parks, in the cafés reminded him of what now seemed a long-lost happiness: couples, children, the distinctive sound of the engine of the first car he had bought her, a woman's gesture, the color of a coat. It was as if his whole existence had been reduced to a series of shuddering jolts, a constant salvo from which he tried to protect himself by averting his gaze. When he looked up at the sky, the shape of the clouds resembled the First Child's scribbles, and he wound up staring at his shoes, at the gutter, or at his lifeline.

———

"Whatever you do, don't go home," his friend R. told him. "Let her get it out of her system. It's up to her to make a choice."

"Friends are coming over Monday night," he replied.

"Don't go home," R. repeated. "No matter what."

They had dinner in a restaurant in Les Halles. R. was having a hard time too. He tried to help, but simply did not have the means. "My problems are nothing compared to yours," R. suddenly said as he thrashed about. "Let's stick with you."

That's the kind of person R. was, the best friend you could have at times like these and the one who later, along with V. and M., would encourage him to turn his notes into a book. "Because it's important not only for you," he said, "but for all of us, for all the men of our generation."

And when he managed to become a working writer again, when all the pronouns turned into characters and the novel grew into a project with form and substance, he would come to believe that he really was writing for the men of his generation as much as for himself. And for the first time in his life he felt a kind of group solidarity with them, to the point of no longer feeling that bond with women, whom he came to hate as much as he had once loved them, as much as he loved them still, because given the right conditions, they were quite capable of using all the weapons of power, a privilege he had thought reserved for the macho imbeciles they had fought so energetically and with such justice in the seventies.

He decides he will not go home yet, the better to go home when the time is right, if it ever should be. He wants her to feel the full weight of his absence. And for her to do that—or rather, for her to do it to his advantage—he must not let her brood upon the blood-cruel images of the many conjugal battles they have not yet fought. She must erase from her memory the tension of past weeks and rediscover a smooth expanse on which, perhaps, he might reappear. He sets himself a deadline: two weeks.

He has lunch with a female friend at La Coupole, and they both recount the sorrows of their love lives. Sometimes parallel lines intersect. As they are leaving the restaurant, they pass a table where a writer he knows is sitting with his ex-wife. They exchange meaningless greetings and he leaves quickly, not wanting to disturb them: they have chosen an out-of-the-way table.

In the street their image returns to him. A man and a woman, lovers not long ago, sitting together again in intimate solitude at a corner table in a restaurant. It occurs to him that she and he ought to try to discover a similar harmony.

He begins dreaming again. Each of us has a life of his own, we lunch together regularly, share a profound tenderness for each other; she tells me her troubles and I tell her mine; we comfort each other; she becomes my best friend.

The scene he pictures is one he knows very well, for it looks just like their lunches together. He decides that viewing things this way is a means of preventing them from changing, or at least of preserving the best part of them.

He reviews the afterlife of the couples he knows who have separated. The worst case is that of his parents, who never saw each other and talked on the phone only exceptionally, when a child had a problem. When he was ten years old his father would drop him off in front of his mother's building for a visit, and she would do the same when she brought his brother or sister. "Brought" was the right word too, because in these conditions the children are packages hauled back and forth, the parents amiable conveyors.

He wants none of that. He knows that the children are an obligatory vector, but he wishes for more. If he lived seven years with this woman, it was because he loved her, and if he loved her, it was also because she was a good person, with a sense of justice he had always admired. She was a person of substance in his life whom he did not want to diminish, and could not diminish, just because they would no longer be sleeping together.

So, he thinks, they will not come together only where the children are concerned. They had been alone when they met, and that former part of themselves had to be kept alive for as long as possible. Separation—if they separated—did not necessarily mean failure. Separation was like a fork in the road from which their paths diverged. They had traveled together for a time, and now one of them was setting off alone. The important thing was *after*, and *after* would depend solely on how they said goodbye for the last time, at the moment of the breakup. They would have to say goodbye, at best tenderly, at worst with some elegance. Then they would take their separate paths, but they would find each other again from time to time, out of pleasure rather than by chance. They would sit at a corner table in a

restaurant, sharing secrets they alone could understand, better than any other man or woman she or
he might be living with. Failure would lie not in
the breakup but in the failure of the breakup.
Separation will be the last act of their life together.

Thinking about it like this makes him feel
strong, almost happy, and he wants to rush to her
to share the plan he has conceived for them. They
would begin immediately. They would find a café,
and he would even touch her hand and she would
not pull away.

But he doesn't rush to her. Instead he walks
along the boulevard, eyes fixed on his shoes because he has just heard a child call its mother.

He also knows that, with rare exceptions, he
has never seen his ex-lovers again. The etiquette
of breaking up is unknown to him. For one thing,
he is too uncomfortable to figure out what to say
or do; when he breaks up with one woman for
another, he quickly draws a line between how he
lived then and how he lives now, the present
opening up into a future that drowns the past in
the ashes of the pluperfect.

For another, breakups are too painful for him
to think about nurturing his pain with insights,
chimeras, and meager remainders. So he simply
flees, almost always for good and all.

This time it would be different. Because she is
the mother of his children. The mother of his

children. He repeats these words and finds them magnificent. Yes, they have given each other that: children.

He spends a night with a girl. In the morning she tells him she slept very badly because he kept touching her body, not so much to make love as to squeeze her tight, to cuddle against her, to hide himself. As though he were seeking comfort in his sleep.

He feels bad too, because this is not the girl with whom he would have liked to wake up. And because no woman seems as beautiful to him as the one who is drifting away.

HE DID NOT LAST THE TWO WEEKS. When he telephoned to hear the First Child's voice, she answered and reminded him of the dinner on Monday evening. "Why don't you come," she said. "It'll be nice." He said no. "You're making a mistake," she objected.

So he went. Rationalization or not, he believed that no strategy could fundamentally alter the shape of the curve now being traced. Had he decided to leave for good, he might have been able to stay away; but he had not made that decision, so home he went. After a two-day trip to nowhere.

It was an insipid evening. He meant to act one way, but instead acted another, as usually happened when he was annoyed. He unclenched his teeth only to mutter the occasional linking device—Oh really? How so? I see!—hoping to sustain a conversation from which he could happily abstain.

He watched her. She was affable, as though nothing had happened. She showed him no tenderness, behaving as matter-of-factly as possible. He decided that she had not taken his departure seriously, that she had always known he would come back, that she had not felt the slightest doubt—or worse, the slightest uneasiness—on that score. If his leaving had been a tactic, it had failed just as surely as all its predecessors. The unaffected ease with which she was changing before his very eyes struck him as an insult, so clearly did it demonstrate that she regarded his decisions as completely insignificant—in which she was not far wrong. After all, he was here, wasn't he?

They spent that night together. "Use the bed if you want," she said. "There's no reason to sleep on the floor!"

Like a dog.

He had dreamed it differently, even knowing the dream was impossible. He had hoped it would be like an incident he had experienced many years ago and of which he still retained a tender memory. One morning he showed up at a female friend's house with a bag of croissants in hand. When he found the lady in bed with a gentleman caller, he tiptoed out as quietly as possible. An hour later she knocked on his door, and they made love more passionately than they ever had.

He fell asleep on the edge of the bed, wearing pajamas, something he never did.

For two days he refused to let her see him naked, grabbing a towel when she came into the bathroom. He got dressed with the door closed. He protected his body, less out of modesty than to make it clear to her that nothing would ever be the same after that thirty-first night.

But everything is the same. As before, she never says goodnight, for fear he might take her in his arms, or good morning, for fear he might want to make love. She slips past him in the hallways, goes through doors ahead of him, calls their bedroom "my" bedroom and the children "my" children, says I don't know whenever he asks her what she's going to do, and speaks of their relationship in the past tense: During the seven years we lived together.

As before, she does her exercises in front of him, gets dressed in front of him, and spends a lot of time looking at herself in the mirror, delighted to be back down to what she weighed "before the First Child."

"You never used to worry so much about your body," he mutters, jealous. Then he leaves the room to avoid hearing her answer.

In normal times she would raise an objection, he another, and she would say, What's the point of arguing, you're always right anyway. All you have to do is look at the facts, he would reply. What facts? she would ask, and he would expound them. Then she would stalk out of the room: You never can resist a scene, can you? He would follow her into the kitchen—You might at least listen to what I have to say—and she would shove a trolley or a pot or a pan and say, What you have to say doesn't make any sense, you poor fool. Furious, he would shout, I hate that, you poor fool shit! Then she would go into the bathroom, and he would follow, defending himself: It's not true I can't resist a scene! She would shake her head with an irritated sneer, and he would say, You really love stuffing me into whatever role suits you. Oh, come on, she would say with a shrug, everyone knows how you are! and he would shout, What about you? Just the other day at . . . Then she would head back into the hallway: The hell with what anyone else thinks, I don't give a shit what anyone else says! He would follow. The hell you don't give a shit! He would give an example, she would go into the bedroom, slamming the door behind her, and he would throw it open: I've had it up to here! You've had it up to here for seven years now! I can't go on like this! he would say, and she would turn to him, sardonic: So leave, you poor fool, leave! And he would leave, for good, going at least as far as the living room, slamming a door in his turn, and then another.

But this time he wants to avoid the usual pattern of escalation. He is determined to control himself. Patience, he repeats to himself again and again. Patience.

He also tells himself, as much for consolation as to prepare for the worst, that he must never forget how hard this woman can be in daily life.

One evening, believing that the situation has reverted to pre-thirty-first-night conditions, he says to her, "Don't ever do that again," referring to that night. She laughs and he wonders, What the hell can I do about it if she does do it again?

He has lunch with M., a writer and screenwriter. The two of them have long had a ritual, showing each other their manuscripts—whether books or screenplays—before publication or shooting. They have complete trust in each other's literary judgment.

Several special memories linked him to M., most especially their participation in antifascist demonstrations. They always ran into each other there.

M. is a man of few words, but very straightforward. Where the children are concerned, he pulls no punches: "If women want to go, let them go. But without the kids. We don't lose the right to see our children grow up just because we're men."

M. pumped him up. Fine, let her move out if that's what she wants to do. But he will keep his sons. And the apartment too, which is theirs.

This resolution gives him an axis, and having adopted a line of conduct, he feels stronger. He finally has a banister to hold on to. Even if he cannot climb back up the stairs he has tumbled down, at least he will stop himself from falling any lower.

"I'll never move out," she replies when he shares his determination with her. "I have no idea what you might be capable of."

He resents this lack of confidence, which leads

her to assume positions designed to protect herself in the event of a breakup: if she moves out, she will also lose the children. But what did she have to protect herself from? If she has forgotten what he is capable of, she might at least remember what he is incapable of!

His parents come to see the children, his mother in the afternoon, his father in the evening. He tries hard, but he doesn't manage to say a word about what is really going on. Simply smiles in the right places, in well-advised acquiescence. The children are amusing, and his mother sticks to her role. He cannot help thinking that, twenty-eight years down the line, his wife and he are about to replay the divorce scene, following a script identical to his parents'. It shakes him deeply to realize that although there had been times when he contemplated leaving his wife, he had never gauged the full weight of the word "divorce." Neither its weight nor its consequences, neither its consequences nor its materiality, neither the act nor the circumstances preceding it. But when his parents come to see him—his mother and her companion, and then his father and his wife—he understands the enormity of the impending tragedy, including its gravity in time, a notion he had not considered until then. And that is why, in spite of all his efforts, he finds himself unable to unclench his teeth.

He managed to fool his mother, but not his father, who telephoned the day after the visit and said, "Something's very wrong. What's going on?"

"Nothing. Lots of work, that's all."

He would keep his explanations to himself for as long as he could, trying to avoid the family pressure, the phone calls and confabs, and, inevitably, the judgments. He would keep them to himself so as to avoid having to account for himself. And also because nothing seemed more horrible to him than the confession he now owed them: I've done exactly what you did.

He works on his novel every night, tranquilized by Valium and three shots of whiskey. It is the day's only livable moment. As he works she sleeps in the next room, behind closed doors.

You're drifting, he tells her.

You're right, she replies.

Careful you don't get swept away.

She laughs tenderly.

She is thinking about the other man, spending her evenings thinking about him. From time to time they speak. One night she says to him, "Most couples who get back together do it for the children."

"In other words," he replies, "if we don't break up we owe it to the children?"

She does not reply. "We'll never do that," he adds.

She has just given him the explanation for the violence she is showing him: she is contemplating the possibility of staying, not for him but for the children. And that, of course, makes her hate him.

Another night she says, "I can't stand this any-more. I'm going to rent an apartment."

"Fine," he says. "But until you get this affair out of your system, until you're settled in, the children stay here."

"I'll never leave without the children."

Often she locks herself in the bedroom and talks on the phone for hours. He closes all the doors between them so as not to hear even a murmur of it. He does not want to encroach on her freedom, and he wants to avoid the diabolical vicious circle of jealousy and its inevitable outgrowths: searches and surveillance. Not only because it is unworthy, but also because the fruits of his discoveries might hurt him even more. He never asks a single question about the other man.

All her old pet names for him are now directed exclusively at the children. Whenever she calls one of his sons by a nickname she had once reserved for him, he flinches, remembering times gone by. He also recalls that long ago she complained that he had given up the pet name he had called her during the first few months that they lived together. He understands the pain she felt then, for now he suffers it himself. The use of diminutives marks a gradation—or degradation —whose scope he measures day by day. When she calls him by his first name, it sounds like the crack of a whip above his head. Meanwhile, he has no idea what to call her anymore. Now and then, driven by habit or by a brief burst of tenderness, they revert to the diminutives of yesteryear, and each time it is a joy and then a wound. As though her tongue were forked, tracing a caress ending in a sting.

————

He likes it when she washes her hair on Saturday for Sunday. He hates it when she washes it on Monday for Tuesday.

He likes it when she pays any kind of attention to him—Your hair's too long, That shirt's no good for you, You're not eating enough.

He hates the sound of her electric epilator, a sinister rumble rumbling for someone else, once a week, from deep in the bathroom. One night he pulls out the plug of the recharger so she won't be able to use it, but then, ashamed, he plugs it back in.

He likes it when she wears clothes that don't suit her, and when she puts on too much makeup or not enough. He feels glad when she complains of a pimple on her skin.

And he hates himself for liking all these things.

Her face changes day by day, no longer glowing with the earlier satisfaction and ecstasy. She now looks tense and hard. The ups and downs of her love affair with the other man frighten him. She is probably weighing what she would lose here and gain elsewhere.

————

He has been living in terror, but it now gives way to smooth, dull shores of sadness. Terror is mobile, sadness stagnant. Like water in a vase.

Often he thinks that he ought to shift the axis of his resolution, forget about winning her back and instead begin the mourning process, thereby preparing himself to lose her. Get one woman out of your system by replacing her with another, they say. But he is out of commission.

HE AWAITED THE FORTIETH DAY with hope, and it was like a fall from a high place. The evening before, she went into the bedroom and closed the door. When he came in, she hurriedly covered a piece of paper she had been writing on. He turned on his heel and left, wondering whether the note was for him or for the other man.

It was for him. In the few lines of this, the only letter she would write him during the entire crisis, she announced that she loved him, that she loved the other man as well, and that she had no plans to leave the house, except the following evening, Tuesday. She would be gone all night and would be home late the next morning. If he had no objection, she would ask her mother to look after the children. That way she wouldn't worry, and neither would he.

He replied, in writing, that it was out of the question to consign care of the children to anyone else on a night their mother intended to sleep elsewhere. The children (he wrote) have a father, and I'll take care of them. All he asked was that she make sure they did not see her leave, and that she bring croissants and flowers with her when she came back the next morning.

He invited some friends over for Tuesday night. A way of celebrating the event, but also of not being alone. "She's spending the night out," was all he told them. "Why don't you come over?"

They spent the day together in the apartment. She was cheerful and animated, happily looking forward to the evening, while he sat slumped in an armchair observing the swell of her obscene joy. But her exhilaration seemed to fade as the hours passed. He realized that his presence was curbing her pleasure, thwarting her spirit. She tried to be tender with him, even made dinner as though she were staying. She probably felt guilty, and she seemed sad to see him like this. But nothing in the world could make her change her plans, and nothing in the world could make her lie to him.

He planned on going out late that afternoon, before his mother-in-law brought the children back. He had no desire to witness either her arrival or the wife's departure. At five o'clock he asked her what the schedule was. "I'm leaving at six," she said.

"What about the children?"

"My mother will be here between six and seven."

He asked her to wait. She refused. "All you care about is your soirée," he said. "You leave me alone with your mother, who doesn't even speak to me. What am I supposed to tell the children?"

"Tell them whatever you want."

She left the room. He followed her into the hallway and asked her to postpone her rendezvous. "Impossible," she said. "I can't reach him now."

He went back to his armchair and waited.

At six o'clock she came over to him.

"I have to go."

She was wearing no makeup and had not changed her clothes. He was glad she had gone to no trouble for the other man, but he wasn't pleased that their relationship had apparently become so settled that she no longer felt the need to get ready for him.

She said goodbye very tenderly. He asked her when she would be back. Before noon, she replied. He hoped she would be earlier. He had calculated the minimum time involved, an evening and a night, but now it was to be part of an evening, a night, and all morning. Before, during, after. I hope I never hurt her the way she's hurting me, he thought. And he told himself that patience was the mother not of all virtue but of masochism.

She left for the second night of her honeymoon.

The mother-in-law arrived a little later. They said a chilly hello and he got the children ready for bed. He stayed with them until they fell asleep. Then he set the table and his guests arrived. He had chosen them because he had known them for a long time and because, for emotional reasons, he felt they were closer to him than to her. He needed some territory of his own. He wanted to have people around, to be taken care of.

When they sat down to eat, he realized that he had inadvertently set an extra place. Everyone laughed at the revealing slip. Then they ate, drank, talked. Finally he asked them what he should do. There was no more talk of patience. The boys said that from this point on he should consider himself at war. The girls agreed, though with some reservations. L. offered a description of the situation as lucid as it was succinct: "Your wife is spending the night with another man. In the meantime she asks you to sit and wait like a good boy. You can't accept that."

P. agreed, and so did the girls. As they all pitched in, they engendered within him a feeling

he had never had until then: pride. Even knowing
how superficial it was, he let the feeling carry him
to new shores, where questions of strategy were
less important than the spirit of pride. It was like
being reborn. He saw himself as a shadow grasping a stone to hurl back at his attacker. A grown-
up. Almost a hero. He told them that he was sick
of all this torture, that he would no longer tolerate
her refusal to decide, that she was hurting him
mercilessly, that she paraded around naked in
front of him, left letters from the other man lying
around, slipped away when he tried to hold her,
and said things like I'm crazy in love, *my* bedroom, *my* children. No, he said, this couldn't go
on any longer.

The more he talked, the more he warmed to the
task, coming ever closer to the relatively more
detached viewpoint of his guests. They listened
eagerly, delighted to see him finally react. Yes,
you're absolutely right, do it, do it. . . .

But do what?

They kicked it around, boisterously toasting
battle plans as they talked. Maybe he should walk
out right now, and take the kids with him. The
morning would be better, said the girls. Okay, but
very early, suggested the boys. I'd leave her a
note, said one of the girls. But with no forwarding
address, advised the boys. No, don't do that, objected the girls. Let her worry a little, said the

boys. But not too much, replied the girls. Put her in peril, yes, but not in danger, argued the girls. And what about him?! thundered P. Don't you think he's in danger? And has been for two months, added L., upping the ante.

That's true, the girls admitted.

Enthused by this new spirit of revolt, he shivered with pleasure at the thought of his wife's coming home with flowers and croissants and finding an empty house. He pictured her going from room to room, looking in vain for children and husband, finally throwing herself abjectly on the couch and bursting into tears: What have I done? What have I done?

And he would return that evening, with great dignity, having taken perfect care of the children. He would come softly to her. Ask her how she was. He would give the Baby and then the First Child his bath, feed them and put them to bed before turning his attention to her. She would crawl into his arms. I was so afraid, she would murmur.

He would not push her away, but he would not embrace her either. Just put a hand on her back, the way she does when he is hurt; and then, since she would want more, he would gently stroke her hair, distant yet present, impressively restrained, without speaking, at least not right away. And later, after she had cried for a long time, he would tell her, It's over now, little girl, it's all over now. . . .

Enveloped in this idyllic image, he suggested an overture meant to avert excessive suffering, but his friends vetoed the idea: You have to stop letting her walk all over you. And he gave in, knowing how right they were even as he knew full well that this was not his style, that if he challenged her to a test of strength he would lose. But he had tried everything else. There was nothing left to lose.

Before his friends left, he made an appointment to meet P. at his place by eleven the next morning.

He got the children dressed and left her a note. He did not say where he was going, only that he would be back that evening.

He arrived at P.'s at eleven sharp. Fifteen minutes later the phone rang. The answering machine was on, but they had turned the volume down. When they played the tape back, there was no message, but he knew it was her. He knew she was worried. He waited ten minutes, then called home. The line was busy. He called R. and S. Their line was busy too. She was calling all his friends, trying to find out where he was.

When he finally got through, he told her. The children are fine, he said. No need to worry. Her voice sounded like it was coming from beyond the grave. He explained that they would be home for dinner, but at three o'clock the prank no longer seemed funny. His pride was gone. At four o'clock he went home.

She was not lying on the couch, there were no flowers or croissants, she did not throw herself into his arms, and if she murmured anything, it was only to say hi.

She was cold and pale, mired in a leaden silence.

He opted for conciliatory lightheartedness and austere amiability. Then, as she gave the children their baths, he wondered which of them was entitled to feel hostile. Anger gripped him when he realized how subtly she had turned the situation to her advantage.

He didn't say a word to her all evening. After the children were put to bed, he asked only whether she wanted to go out for their anniversary the next day. She said no. He told her that from now on, it was war. She shrugged. He explained the rules of the game as he saw them: he would never abandon the house or the children; he had given up trying to win her back and would now fight her inch by inch until the situation was resolved. "I'm not going to war against you, but for myself," he concluded. "Because I can't stand my own passivity anymore, and because if I don't react, I'll drown."

She said nothing.

He went upstairs to see his friend on the fourth floor.

The next day he proposed the first truce: he had flowers sent to her office for their seventh anniversary. He asked that they be delivered as soon as possible.

At eleven o'clock she had not called. At noon he telephoned the delivery service and got confirmation that the roses had been sent. At one o'clock he got confirmation from her office that they had been delivered. He asked to speak to her and was told that she was not at her desk. He waited until after lunch, then decided to give her one more chance, till four. When that deadline passed, he picked up the phone and called her private line, pretending he needed some information, which she duly gave him. "Did you get my flowers?" he then asked, as offhandedly as possible.

"Yes."

Silence.

"Are they pretty?"

"Yes."

"What time did they get there?"

"Ten."
Silence.
"You could have at least given me a call."
"I was going to."
Silence.
He hung up.

The next day he had lunch with K., one of his screenwriter friends. "There's no point in fighting it," she said. "In cases like this men always wind up tossed out and paying child support. In addition to which, women take advantage of the situation to demand anything they can get. They figure it's due them, since the whole thing is the man's fault anyway."

"But that's disgusting."
"It's worse than disgusting. It's unfair."
He thought K. was exaggerating.
She wasn't.

ON THE MORNING OF THE FORTY-
fourth day, eager to escape the war, he
decided to go away with the First Child.
He talked to the boy and telephoned his friends in
the south, telling them he would set out the following evening. Then he informed her of his plan.
"Why do you want to go away?" she asked.

"Because we can't go on like this. You have to
go do your thing with the other man and then
decide."

"Why are you taking the First Child?"

"Because I need him."

There was another reason too: leaving the
house with his son was not desertion and therefore
did not violate his line of conduct.

She raised no objection. At that time she still
felt guilty.

His father called and said he wanted to take the
children the following weekend. "Not possible,"

he replied. "I'm going somewhere with the First Child."

"What's going on?"

"You were right the other day. I've got problems. I have to see you."

He needed to talk to his father. In the course of this general rout he had run through every one of his friends, and now he wanted a different view, from someone who could offer him something other than the sadness, solidarity, and enormous attentiveness his family of the heart had given him. What he needed now was support—he had to let himself go, and he wanted to be treated like a child.

But his father did not see him as a child. In his father's eyes he saw grief, a kind of lassitude, and enormous powerlessness. He told himself that he was old, and that his father was very old. They had an adult talk about an adult situation that one of them had faced twenty-eight years ago and the other had only just now discovered. They were joined by the plinth of experience, which they were now able to mount together. But no more than that.

The present situation was especially painful to him in that he felt caught between the hammer of his own breakup with his wife and the anvil of his parents' divorce. Disjointed images ran together in his mind, forming a whirlwind in which he felt lost, forcing him to deal simultaneously with this affront to his maturity and with childhood's ancient stings. It was as though he had assumed too many personae at the same time: himself today, the little boy he was long ago, his father, his sons. Sometimes when he thought of his wife, he would see his mother, and his image of the other man sometimes dissolved into the face of his late stepfather, the object of that earlier separation. He could not shake the thought that his parents had broken up at just about the age he was now, and he contemplated with horror the prospect of reproducing a mechanism whose very repetition made it seem ineluctable. Like destiny.

In the past two months he had had all the time in the world to measure the full power of the hammer. With his father he wanted to talk about the anvil. Only he could help him free himself of the iron of childhood.

But his father did not understand that. Or if he did, he refused to follow the script. Probably out of modesty, perhaps out of fear, having suffered too much to relive age-old humiliations through his son's present sorrows. But most of all because, having made a new life for himself, he had turned that old page of his history forever.

His father was working in his office when he arrived, and asked him to sit not on the other side of the desk but alongside him. These gestures and attentions roused a buried memory that now rose to the surface of his mind. It was as though he had reassumed a chair he had occupied more than two decades ago.

He is fourteen years old, and in love for the first time. He tells his father, who shows him to a seat in his office and then utters this delightful proposition: "Would you like a cigar?"

As they smoke, the father talks about his own life and his past mistresses, and he gives his son a piece of perfectly respectable advice: "Get laid as much as you can."

Between billows of smoke and repeated coughing fits, the kid replies that he will do his best.

He and his father have talked twice in their life: when he was fourteen and when he was seventeen. The first encounter was tinged with the cigar of awkward intimacy; the second marked a fissure he had never wanted.

He is seventeen and ready to move out. His things are packed up in the bedroom. His father does not want him to go. They are alone in the apartment, isolated by the dark and the sleep of the others. His father does not want him to go. All night long, until dawn, he tries to convince him not to do it. The son struggles to break away as gently as possible, so as not to cause hurt. He loves his father. Loves him passionately.

But he won't stay. Never has this man of forty —solid, discreet, barded with all the masculine weapons of his generation's arsenal—never has he opened up like this, expressing so overtly an affection that his father and his father's father and all the fathers of the era when males were supposed to rule, without ever weakening or laying themselves bare, had learned to express only through paternity's external signs.

But he will not stay. Blame it on '68. What the adolescent wants is to broaden his field of vision, to walk out on the family and into life itself, to cultivate fields on his own. He has to win his freedom. But where he sees continuity, the father sees a sundering. The son is cutting the cord. Yet the depth of their complicity will remain indelible: at ten the child chose to live with his father, who has instilled in him moral and ethical values to which he will always cling. In May they stood together on the same side of the barricades, in their hearts if not in the streets.

Nevertheless, he will not stay. For after May came September, when everything fell apart. Three of them had ridden this merry-go-round together—he, his father, his stepmother—and now one was staying on while the others got off. Two years later the child still dreamed of the queasy nervousness he felt when the man checked his report cards. And that's what they talk about that night, telling each other secrets, speaking lacerating words. For the first time his father admits that he has often been wrong, that it hurts him that his son is leaving. He exposes a part of himself that subsequent generations will no longer seek to conceal: the feminine side that every man carries within himself.

At dawn they separate, loving each other as never before. Before closing the door to his room, the father says, "When I wake up I'll find out what you've decided to do."

When he wakes up, the son is gone.

Now they sit side by side in the office, and the father nods sadly. He acts as he always has: generous, upright, unimpeachable. But what the son needs is not a figurehead but a magician. He wishes his father could settle all his problems with a wave of his magic wand, just as he used to do. He wishes he could make them all see reason—his wife, himself, the other man. But he isn't a child, and his father is no longer a wizard. He can't do anything. He can't do anything at all.

So the son becomes a father speaking to his

children's grandfather. He passes the baton to his sons. "I want you to be a part of my boys' lives," he says.

Then he stands up, kisses his father goodbye, and leaves. He would now travel a road he had often taken in the past, the route of ancient miseries: he would head south.

H E HAS COME THIS WAY A HUNDRED times before: hitchhiking alone on the spur of the moment, hitchhiking in organized groups, driving his first cars, at least one of which died on the edge of a field beside this road. Then later in powerful, well-heated sedans, and the last few times by plane.

The south is his most secret continent. When he was single it was his refuge whenever anything went wrong in his life, which meant about three times a year. He went less for the sea, the sky, and the pines, all of which left him indifferent, than for his friends, many of whom were just as broke as he had been at twenty.

His favorite haunts were those of the painters of Saint-Tropez. Not the lords of the galleries, but the dilettantes of the port. Having sold records and apartments, painted numbers on parking spaces, sped from office to office in Paris as a messenger, and shuffled papers in the administration building at the Sorbonne, he had finally landed at the place du Tertre, where he sold third-rate canvases painted by others but which, necessities of place having their own implacable logic, he claimed as his own. His painter-employers were his comrades, and he often joined them in the south, where they emigrated during the high season.

They formed a clique. Most of them drove old Meharis, the richest a classic Jaguar. They carried monkeys on their shoulders, shoplifted, threw improbable parties, made scenes in restaurants, slept with girls, and finished last night's champagne at breakfast the next morning.

He was the rookie of the group, and he admired these artists, who seemed to have come straight out of *Scènes de la vie de bohème*. He loved their creative rigor, their tirades against the bourgeoisie, their (theoretical) rejection of compromise. With them he relived his schoolboy pranks and discovered the drunkenness of nights that never end.

As time went on, however, he grew apart from them and finally lost touch. At thirty-five they had seemed triumphant, but by forty-five bitterness set in. The alcohol was diluted, the painting had languished. He didn't like them anymore. Times had changed.

Later, when he returned to the south, it was in

search of a niche of asylum with different friends whom he had known since adolescence: J. and A. and their four children.

They were a kind of fixture in his existence. They had met in high school and had been radical activists during the same period. Later their paths diverged, but not their aspirations. He wanted to write, and he did. They wanted a sea change, and they got it. Of all his old friends from the days of rallies, demos, and street battles, they alone preserved the lifestyle honored by the vagabonds of that era. They admired one another for the energy they had expended so relentlessly, from adolescence onward, to attain the goals they had set for themselves.

J. and A. were his absolute opposites, which was why he felt the need to see them when nothing was going right: he was drifting into an existence he no longer recognized, receiving images no one else could send back to him.

He drives toward them now feeling just as lost as he did at twenty. But things are not the same; far from it. Now, a little boy of five—his son—lies asleep in the backseat.

He looks at him in the rearview mirror. The boy is stretched out on the seat, his toys and stuffed animals scattered around him.

They had talked a lot during the trip, without ever touching on the problem of the *vorce*. It was as if, having left Paris, they had decided to drift aimlessly together, fleeing pressure, ensconced in this warm car, crossing snow-covered surfaces that would lead them to an oasis where, he hoped, they would find peace.

They arrive in the evening. A large house on the edge of the Berre marsh. He goes inside and puts down his baggage, literally and figuratively. He breathes more freely. Everything is different here. His friends are virgins: they know nothing about the crisis.

This is a roost where children rule. The First Child plays with the others, while he sits in the kitchen with A. and J. and tells them everything. He feels as though he is emptying himself, but it is only a feeling. The truth is he's charging his friends with an energy for which he can find no release. So he transmits it instead. In return, during the week he will spend here they will transmit waves identical to his own: he will receive a piece-meal account of the debacles this couple, too, has faced. Not for the first time, as he compares tales, he decides that his own has not attained the heights from which a fall is inevitable. From this he will draw fresh hope.

He had forgotten just one detail: all of his friends who managed to reweave their suddenly severed threads had known one another since adolescence. The others, the ones who lacked such long and seasoned intimacy, had fallen on the field of honor.

The first night they threw a party. Boys and girls in their early twenties showed up, wearing the same kind of clothes and speaking and laughing just as they had at that age. They listened to Higelin and Cabrel, smoked joints, and went to bed very late. Before going to sleep he made a date with one of the girls.

He sleeps with his son. When he wakes up, he sees the boy standing at the living room window, silently staring out at the sea. He calls him. The child comes over and asks, "Daddy, can we play pirates?"

He gets up and takes him to the rocks.

When A. gives her little girl her bottle, he turns away. Though he has no trouble playing with the other children, who are much older than his own, he is quite incapable of taking any interest in the smallest, who is just a little younger than the Baby. When he looks at them he sees not A. and her child but his wife and his second son. When J. is there he sees not a father and a mother touched by their baby but himself, her, and his baby as they could have been but would never be again.

When they hold the little girl out to him, he takes her at arm's length and looks around for someone to pass her to. He just can't. Simply cannot.

One after another his friends phone. He had told no one he was leaving, and they are worried. They want to know how he is. These calls prevent him from clearing his head. Something he would not manage to do in any event.

He spends his days in front of the fireplace, adding wood to the fire with his son. He thinks of nothing but the Baby and his mother. You can travel six hundred miles, but your head goes with you. He knew that, but he had come nonetheless. He wants his wife, so many miles to the north, to meet the other man, to see him night and day, and to make up her mind once and for all.

But she doesn't meet him. When they talk on the phone, she says, "I'm not going out," even though he doesn't ask a single question about how she is spending her time.

She calls every day. He would prefer not to talk to her, but the First Child invariably hands him the receiver: "Daddy, it's Mommy."

Sullen, he answers.

One morning she reminds him that they have reservations for New Year's at a bungalow in a vacation center. He says he sees no point in going away together. She insists. He asks her how long this farce will go on. She hesitates, pauses for a moment, and declares, I don't know. A long silence, and then he asks whether she still loves him. She says she does.

When the girl he had asked out calls to confirm the meeting place, he cancels. He decides he would rather sleep with his son than with a woman. In any case, he does not have the strength for the obligatory games of seduction. He would have happily jumped straight into bed with her and jumped straight out afterwards, but what was the point of that kind of humiliation with someone he didn't know and to whom he had nothing but that to propose?

He watches his son sleep in the sun. His eyelids are so incredibly fragile, translucent. He kisses them softly. He thinks to himself that he could never live without this child.

He is cutting the First Child's nails. Suddenly the little boy draws back his hand, lowers his head, and says, "Daddy, I'm sad."

He puts his arms around him.

"Why are you sad, little man?"

"Because I'm leaving my nails."

He has never been authoritarian with his son. The mother often chides him for this, and he knows she is right. But he believes that she is capable of compensating for his excesses and deficiencies, as he is capable of compensating for hers. It makes for a balance based on the complementariness of the adults. He dares not think of how his children would develop if that balance were broken.

One day the First Child announced that he wanted to learn music. He took him to a class and stood in the back of the room to assess the quality of the lesson. The teacher had the pupils sit in a

semicircle around him. Then he distributed per-
cussion instruments, and the children began to
play. The teacher interrupted them constantly,
telling them to do this or that, correcting the
positioning of their fingers, asking one child to
hit louder and another to move somewhere else:
"No, not here, there—not there, here—hurry up,
will you!"

After five minutes of this the First Child turned
to his father and called out, very loud, "Daddy,
can we go now?"

They left the room hand in hand.

Later the boy decided he wanted to learn the cello.
The father rented an instrument and asked a music
teacher to come to the apartment. He sat in on a
few lessons. It lasted three months. His son agreed
to do what the teacher asked, provided the teacher
would also do whatever he asked the child to do.
During the last lesson, he said, "I'm gonna sing
the Batman song for you, and you sing it after
me."

The child grabbed the bow and ran it noisily
across the strings, hollering, "Bat-man! Bat-man!"

And the teacher repeated "Bat-man!" an octave
lower, on his eighteenth-century instrument.

The father collapsed into uncontrollable laughter. The teacher left, and that was the end of the cello lessons.

He always backed his son up. When he was small, the boy was a slow, hesitant talker. A stutterer. Every time he tried to say a sentence, his father would silence all surrounding conversations to allow the child to express himself. He had never stopped talking since.

He backed him up because he believed that a child is always right against adults. Which was obviously wrong. But it was at least partly thanks to his attitude that the First Child was so brazen, so frank, determined, and natural. All good qualities, he felt. The task of correcting the excesses cultivated by the father always fell to the mother. He dared not think of how his children would develop if that balance were broken.

He asked the First Child no questions, but the First Child said, "I want to stay with Mommy."

That hurt. He thought about it for an entire day, discussed it with A. and J. That evening he called the mother and said, "The First Child wants to stay with you. We're coming home tomorrow. You can have the apartment. I'll move out."

She told him she wouldn't be in tomorrow. "I offer you everything," he shouted, anger scorching his voice, "and you can't even be bothered to take it! I'm not going to sacrifice myself for nothing!"

She replied that in any case he changed his mind so often that she had given up trying to follow him.

He hung up on her.

"It's war again," he told A. and J. "But this time it's the final conflict." He was just showing off. Trying to draw force from a show of force.

The First Child came looking for him. "Daddy," he said, "I thought it over and I want to stay with you."

An hour later: "Daddy, I thought some more and I want to be with my brother."

He phoned her again. She called V., then R.

V. called him, then R., then she called again.

She called A.

G. called him. Then P. Then L.

A. talked to him.

R. called back.

He called S.

N. called. Then she called again. Then his father.

He went out for a walk.

She called back late that evening. "Let's calm down and discuss it when you get back to Paris."

He stayed another two days in the house at the Berre marsh. Then he kissed his friends and their children goodbye and set out for Aix-en-Provence, where he would meet his friend C. and her daughter.

He had known C. for twenty years. She was like his kid sister, and he like her big brother. Or sometimes the other way around, depending on who needed the other more.

Today it is his turn. She is waiting for him at a table in the café they used to meet in when he came down from Paris to see her. She watches him come in, carrying his sleeping son in his arms. They smile at each other. They have not seen each other in several years, but so deep is their intimacy, so many the misfortunes they have been through together, so great the tenderness with which they love each other, that when he sits down it is as though he has recovered his rightful place. His place beside her.

They stroll arm in arm along the Cours Mirabeau. The First Child walks up ahead with C.'s daughter. It's a beautiful day. The city is ochre. He remembers his wife, long ago, walking with him on this tree-lined avenue, luminous and laughing, impish and flirtatious, having no other role to play than her own—freed of the constricting garb of her working life.

"If my wife and I separate," he tells C., "I'll come live here."

They talk about relationships. Couples always make plans. They start by wanting to love each other. Then they try to live together, then to have children. Later on they plan for trips, vacations, weekends, dates, and parties. Finally, when it's all gone and they don't know how to bring it back, they dream about the evening meal.

"And neither one of us likes to cook," he says.

———

"Would you really leave Paris?" C. asks.

He says he would. He would rent a big house near the sea where his children could come, even his wife if they managed to get along. C. and her daughter could live there too. Other friends too, if they wanted. He would work in the sun. They would be far from the madding crowd.

He builds an ideal universe in his imagination, really no more than the shady slope of a peak he prefers not to descend. He begins to fall in love with the sea, the gulls, the umbrella pines, and he applies them, like so many palliatives, to new situations he is ready to conceive of only now, two months into the crisis. For the first time he speaks of his wife and their life together in the past tense.

They take the First Child to a café, to a restaurant, on the merry-go-round, and to the bakeries. The boy is happy. Nobody makes him do anything: whatever he wants, he gets. The father feels it is the least he can do, things being what they are.

That evening he goes out alone with C. Since they saw each other last she has gotten her driver's license and bought a small car. She shows it to him proudly, opening the door and getting behind the wheel, perched on two cushions that allow her to see the road. "They shouldn't give licenses to little girls less than three feet tall," he says, laughing.

She gives him a good-natured punch, and they set out. They make the rounds of all the clubs but don't feel comfortable in any of them. They get back in the car. "Look what a good driver I am!" C. says, going sixty miles an hour.

He objects that when the roads are icy, little girls less than three feet tall would do better to be taking their naps.

"Is there ice?"

He teaches her how to engine-break, how to use the windshield wipers and directional signals, how not to pass on the right and to slow down in town. By the time they get back to downtown Aix, they are laughing like kids. He hasn't taken Valium in two days.

They wind up in a café packed with students where they have to shout to be heard. He tells her about the time he kissed a sixteen-year-old girl on the mouth, but that was as far as he went, because after all . . . "How?" she asks. "Like this," he replies.

He kisses her on the mouth. She sits back in her seat and laughs. "Don't go too far now!"

He takes her by the neck, she offers him her lips, they kiss, and they are happy.

"How come you never wanted to sleep with me?" he asks.

"But we did sleep together!"

"Sleep, yeah. But that's all."

"Because you're like my brother."

That night he has a feeling they could do it. But they don't. First of all because she might not agree, but also because he does not want his son to wake up in the morning and find him sleeping with a woman who is not his mother.

They kiss again and separate. He is not her brother, and she is not his sister. He loves their loving friendship passionately.

On the last morning they are awakened by the telephone. The First Child leaps out of bed and answers. It is his mother. "We're not coming home today," he says. "We're coming home in—" he counts on his fingers—"in four days."

Then he calls his father. "Daddy, it's Mommy."

He stops laughing. Takes the receiver. "When are you coming back?" she asks.

"When the First Child wants to."

"No. Enough already. I want to see you."

He is silent.

"Both of us? You mean you want to see *him*, right?"

"I would like you all to be here."
He closes his eyes.
"Did you hear me?"
"Okay. We'll be there late this afternoon."

He takes his first Valium in Orange, his second in Lyon, his third in Auxerre. By the time they get to Paris, the box is empty. He stops at a pharmacy. He is afraid to see her.

H E THOUGHT HE WOULD KNOW AT the very first gesture, and so he did: she opened the door, kissed the First Child, then kissed him, her hands clasped behind his neck, a peck on the left cheek and one on the right, her face carefully turned from his to make sure their lips did not meet.

He took another quarter-dose of Valium.

The First Child gave his brother the stuffed animal they had bought for him in Aix. The three of them played on the living room rug. Then he sat down in an armchair across from her, holding the Baby on his lap. They talked about rain and seasons, children, friends, and work. He was dying to smoke. He sensed that she was as tense as he was. Both of them made every effort to maintain goodwill.

He held out for a quarter of an hour, then went

to the window, filled a pipe, and lit it, taking care that the billows of smoke wafted out the window. Then, since it was very cold, he closed the window most of the way, letting it rest on the catch. When he decided that the bulk of the smoke was gone, he went back to his seat, hugging the walls so as not to come too close to her.

He sat down and smiled at her, taking quick puffs on his pipe and blowing the smoke discreetly off to the side. She spoke no word of complaint, and he thought the game was won.

He was wrong. Suddenly she stood up and opened every window in the room as wide as possible. He cupped his pipe in the palm of his hand. Cold swept through the apartment.

He looked at the ceiling.

She went out into the hallway, then came back and shouted, "That pipe stinks! At least I wasn't cold when you were away!"

"So leave!" he screamed.

"That's exactly what I'm doing! I've been looking for an apartment for the past three days."

And it all began again.

On the second night she says, "I'm looking for something in the neighborhood. It'll be easier for the children."

"You're not taking the children."

"I'm taking the Baby. He's too young to live without his mother."

"I'll keep the First Child."

She is silent for a moment, then replies, "Not all the time."

"How much, then?"

She hesitates. But he knows she has already thought it out. "You can have him five days a week," she finally says. "I'll take him the other two."

You can't separate the children, his friends tell him.

If she agrees I'll keep both of them, he replies.

She doesn't.

The third night: "Will you help me with the deposit on my new apartment?"

He says nothing.

"Can I have an answer?"

"I thought you didn't want anything from me. Livry-Gargan isn't good enough for you anymore?"

"Why should I have to move to Livry-Gargan just because I spent two nights with my lover?"

He cannot stand that word. Neither the word nor the way she uses it, with that mixture of pride and provocation that forces him to see with no possible detour, to hear with no possible dissimulation, and to understand with no way out. A word that is not in their lexicon. She hurls it at him as though he were someone else, an older person with whom she had a different history and who would take it in a different way. It was the kind of thing she might have said to her father, affecting that very same tone and inflection, with the insolence of an adolescent defying an authority figure who might respond to her defiance with a slap in the face—something he had never done, neither to her nor to any other woman, and which he would not do, and not only because he was not her father.

The fourth night: "If you want to know the truth, it's all over between my lover and me, but I'm moving out anyway."

"Why?"

"Because I'm sick of living alongside a man. What I want is to live *with* him."

He tries to talk to her, to reason with her, but it doesn't work. She is stubborn and nasty, obstinate and cruel.

The fifth night: "Can you tell me if you'll give me any money for the Baby?"

"No!" he shouts.

"Bastard!"

"Asshole!"

He leaves, slamming the door on his way out.

He arms himself for battle because he can find no other solid ground to stand on. He is not at the same point she is, adding up all the grievances of their life together. Maybe later he would come to that, in self-defense. But for the moment the complete absence of tenderness, intimacy, and gestures of affection fortifies his will. He joins the war she is waging against him, using the same crude weapons and the same ammunition, firing back with anything that comes to hand. In fact, he now wants this war, which, by fueling his anger, shields him from more vulnerable emotions. He wants it the better to hate her, the better not to love her anymore, so that no feeling, no desire, no trifling memory can weaken him. Whenever she proposes a half-truce with a silence or a vaguely amiable word, he spurns it. Never again, he says to himself. If he had been willing to agree to anything before, it was because he thought peace possible. I don't know, I don't know, I don't know. Well, now she knows, and so does he. Now he wants to force her to go all the way: to break up, to move out, to leave him the First Child.

The sixth night: "You're after my ass because I'm the only man you can lash out at. I'm carrying the can for all the others."

"What an idiot."

"Otherwise we'd be able to separate without all this violence."

"Just leave. Then there won't be any more violence."

The seventh day: "I know what you want," he says.

"You always know everything."

"You want me to move out."

"You might think about it, yes. . . ."

"Anything else?"

"It would be only natural, after all. Why should I be the one to leave?"

Rage. "In the end you'll forget everything. You'll make me the son of a bitch responsible for all this bullshit."

"I don't feel like talking to you."

"Look, I know plenty of women who've left

their men. They went without asking for a thing. But you want it all, and a clear conscience to boot."

She walks out. He follows. She asks him which women he has in mind.

He gives names. "Just like you!" she screams. "Always dragging other people into everything! Forget about everyone else! Why don't you ask X. what she thinks?"

"Yeah, and why don't you ask Y.?"

As usual, when they run out of arguments they appeal to a higher, ostensibly objective, authority: their friends.

"Will you remember to put the First Child's snack in his backpack?"

"Yeah."

"He gets out at four-thirty."

"Thanks."

"And don't forget—"

"I'm his father. I know what I'm supposed to do!"

"I wonder!"

That morning they divvy up the time devoted to the children the way they used to quantify the hours spent on household chores. I'll be home at six, you don't take him to school, who's going to give him his breakfast?

He is exhausted.

He refuses to accept the exemplary role she tries to assume whenever they talk about the boys. He refuses to accept her attempt to reduce him to an ephemeral presence in his children's lives. In the old days, when all was well between them, she always used to marvel at what a good father he was. But now collapse is near, and he feels she is trying to pitch her tent on maternal ground she pretends he has never shared, trying to consign him to the rut men were mired in during the sixties. As if some sort of innate principle dictated that the mother is responsible for everything while the father is just a kind of spare room in the edifice of child rearing. And of course that way of looking at things exposes the father's true nature: uninterested, clumsy, and irresponsible. As the danger of separation draws closer, the division of tasks pales before the division of roles, itself heralding the division of children.

They are in a department store. She is fifteen yards ahead of him, and suddenly she turns and calls out: "Hey man!"

He freezes.

"You coming?"

He walks after her. No more pet name, no more first name, no more intimate identity at all. From this point on he is Hey man!

Ex-baby, ex-honey, ex–my guy. Henceforth Hey man! Thus would she avert slipping back in time in the history of their life together, where too great an intimacy lurked, while also avoiding the whip crack of his bare first name, which she never used, even when talking about him in the third person.

Hey man! If hypocorism is a measure of the temperature of love, he is dangerously close to absolute zero.

One evening he goes out walking and loses his keys. As he stoops to scan the sidewalk, a passerby turns around and walks back toward him. "Hey man!" he calls out.

He stops and looks up.

"Lose something?"

"Yeah," he says. "My wife."

HIS FIRST FILM AND HIS LATEST
book were released at the same time, one in
the theaters, the other in the bookstores. It
should have been a great moment, but his heart
wasn't in it. He gave interviews, had his picture
taken, appeared on radio and television. But this
not at all unpleasant time of minor glory, coming
after months of lonely labor, left him unmoved.

To his audience he looked like a writer on the
way up, but in his own mind he was a man on the
skids. Celebrated in public, shattered within. He
was late to appointments with journalists and did
not even read his reviews. He was completely
unable to reconcile the external fires with the red
lantern in whose glow he was wasting away.

He sits with V. at a table stacked with hundreds
of copies of their book. They are signing press
copies.

"You can't go on like this," V. says.

"Why not?"

"Look at you!"

He is pale. He has lost a little over twenty pounds in two months.

"Get a lawyer and get a divorce."

Late that morning his wife drops in to say hello, and they sign a copy of the book for her. *To my future ex-wife*, he writes, *with all my heart*.

V. jokes with her, but he does not look at her. He thinks of the four earlier books he published during their time together. He had never inscribed any of them with as much sadness as this one.

"She doesn't look so great either," V. says after she leaves. "Maybe you should try to work things out."

He thinks about that.

"If she came, it's because she still has feelings for you," V. says.

He explains that it has been like that from the beginning: a positive sign, then a negative one. He never knows whether he's coming or going, and he can't take it anymore.

Then he asks the eternal question, which a hundred others have heard before: "You think it's over?"

V. shakes his head. "I think it's worth a try. At least call a Christmas truce for the children."

They eat lunch separately in the same restaurant, each with a female friend. He likes this one a lot. One night they had shared wine and dances at a party, and afterwards a bed. Her name is N. She is funny, slightly cynical, charming, and very beautiful.

She has been living with a man for six months, and she misses her nights off. They play a game, grading her companion: he is cultured (20 out of a possible 20), has no sense of humor (1/20), and is not bad as a partner (15/20). He is jealous (5/20), very loving (18/20), and loyal (10/20). They assign coefficients, multiply and divide, and come up with a mediocre overall score: 11/20.

"Should I leave him?" N. asks.

"Right away," he replies.

They drink to it.

He thinks to himself that he ought to play the same game about his wife, then realizes that he can cheat by assigning whatever coefficients he wants. But however it came out, he knew he would grant her a prize and the jury's congratulations.

After lunch they join V. again. Several other friends arrive, and they drink to the new book. A whole group of them wind up on the rue des

Saints-Pères, having cracked a case of champagne which they propose to consume by drinking to the health of the first publishers whose offices they come upon.

At the first stop they burst into a room where the reading committee is meeting, interrupting the session and once again drinking to the fortunes of the new book.

Late in the afternoon he and V. finally land in a bar, where they empty a couple of bottles of Bordeaux, drinking to the fortunes of the new book. "Call a Christmas truce," V. repeats. "Promise me you will."

He promises.

At six o'clock they call their publisher to apologize for not finishing the press copies. He has been looking for them everywhere. One by one, colleagues of the publisher push open the door of the bar to take a quick glance at the unedifying spectacle of two authors who prefer drinking Pauillac to signing books.

As he turns off the rue des Saints-Pères, tottering on his motorbike, V. calls out after him, "Don't forget—you promised!"

He speeds down the boulevard Saint-Germain. Two cops on motorscooters suddenly flank him. He smiles at them. They motion to him, and he waves. He beams. One of them points at his head. He raises his hand to his bare skull, laughs, then shouts: "No, I don't have a helmet! No helmet at all!"

It occurs to him that alcohol and no helmet make a nice combination. Drink or drive. Okay, he's doing both, but he doesn't give a fuck. If my wife has to come and get me at the station, he thinks to himself, she'll have to speak my name. I'm here to bail out Hey man!

But the cops laugh and disappear. A good sign, he says to himself.

When he gets home, he sleeps for an hour, then stays with the children until their mother comes home. He sits down with her in the living room, closes the door, and says, "I have a proposition for you."

The alcohol has sapped his taste for warfare. What he really wants is to ask her to stay and to try again. Wipe the slate clean and start from scratch. But she seems so cold, so solidly walled up in her concrete bunker, that he is sure that only her pride will speak today. He also remembers that she never lowers her guard when he proposes a truce after a fight. In the old days she was miraculously expert at defusing his anger: she would laugh at him, poke fun at him. She has an impressive facility for not taking his weaknesses seriously. He adores the ease with which she has always been able to help him, through her humor, to avoid assuming a role he hated.

But for a long time now she has been responding tit for tat. Sometimes she even starts it, issuing a provocation, then withdrawing when he responds. He cannot stand the way she strikes her colors and then refuses to let him speak. When she does that he follows her from room to room, and her flight aggravates his exasperation until the targets of his resentment proliferate: the original cause, doubled by the evasion, tripled by a dart hurled on the fly, quadrupled by a reply that elicits a fresh salvo. The shouting matches escalate, rising from one level to the next, even as both of them forget the cause of the outburst.

But today he wants peace. He begins by walking on tiptoe, tossing out bait he hopes she will devour avidly: he agrees to go away to the cottage they had planned to rent for New Year's. She doesn't budge. Just sits stiff and severe on the edge of her armchair. He beats a retreat. "Let's call off the war."

"I'm not fighting a war," she replies.

"Look," he says, dodging that shot, "we've been trying to leave each other for two months and haven't been able to do it."

She acquiesces.

"I'm proposing a truce."

"What kind of truce?"

"Christmas. For the kids."

"I guess it's the least we can do."

He tries to gain an extra week. "Christmas and New Year's."

"Okay."

"After that we'll see."

"We'll see, yes."

He dreams of lighting his pipe, but holds back. He smiles at her. She doesn't look at him.

"I'd like to propose something else as well. . . ."

She makes a three-quarter turn in the chair. She is wearing new pantyhose and a new pair of shoes. "I like your shoes," he says.

She extends a leg. "I bought them from a girl-friend. Not bad, huh?"

"Terrific, really."

"Four hundred francs . . . pretty good, huh? She only wore them once."

"Very nice."

"Worth it, don't you think?"

"Four hundred francs? Are you kidding?"

She stands up.

"Wait a minute, I'm not finished."

"What?"

"I was saying I had something else to propose."

"Oh yeah."

She goes to the door and leans against the jamb.

"Listen. . . ."

He finds it hard to talk. He wishes she would sit down, that she wouldn't stand there like that, her hand on the doorknob, ready to lam it.

If he asks her to stay and try again, she will walk straight out of the room. I don't know I don't know I don't know. He changes course.

"We could try to postpone the breakup. Just for the kids."

She watches him very closely.

"We always said we would never stay together for the children, but we owe it to them to try at least. The least we can do, don't you think?"

"I don't know."

"Let's try to live together for a few months. Till June, for example. If we make it, great. If not, we'll get a divorce. Calmly."

"You, calm?"

He refuses to bite.

"If we can't manage to work it out in six months, then we'll know a break is inevitable. Then we'll do it elegantly, instead of sordidly. What do you think?"

She is still staring at him. He looks into her eyes.

"Well?"

"I'll think about it."

She leaves.
He lights his pipe.

The next day she gives him no answer, nor the day after that, nor in the days that follow. But two nights before Christmas she says, "I broke the earrings you gave me last Easter. If you can find the same ones again . . ."

If he could find the same ones! He would have combed the earth looking for them.

He telephones all his friends with the news. "She asked me for a pair of earrings. You don't ask a man for a pair of earrings when you're about to leave him. She's staying!"

He is sure she is going to give him the six months he asked for. And if she stays six months, that means she's willing to let him win her back. And if she's willing to let him win her back, then he will win her back, and if he does that, then he saves his family. I've won! he thinks to himself.

He did his Christmas shopping in a state of euphoria. Champagne for Mom and Dad, presents for everyone! When she suggested that they exchange presents on Christmas morning instead of

Christmas Eve, he agreed: Fine, we'll do it in the morning. When she wanted to invite friends of hers over the next day, he said, Fine, they're more than welcome! When she decorated the tree alone with the children, without him, he swallowed his disappointment and rejoiced at the ornaments and the tinsel. He gave her everything she wanted. Yes, he was sure he had saved his family.

On Christmas Eve he went off Valium.

But she was sad. Christmas was morose, like a tree with drooping boughs. They pretended to be having a fine old time, but they were each preoccupied with their own thoughts. She admitted that she was mourning her breakup with the other man. It wasn't easy, she said. He understood. He understood everything. He tried to be tender but unobtrusive. He avoided kissing her. At night he did not touch her. He looked at her, loved her, and waited for her to come back to him. He dreamed of tucking her in like a little girl.

They went to the movies again. He sat straight in his seat, arms folded, magnificently resisting the temptation to take her hand but managing to make sure that their shoulders touched, just to remind her he was there. The fingers of his left hand rested on his own forearm. He stretched them out so that she could touch them if she felt the urge.

And she did. Just a quick light touch, but still . . . He felt warm. He felt good. He leaned closer to her and whispered, "Do you think we'll ever make love again the way we used to?"

"Yes," she said.

He dreamed of taking her like a virgin.

They leave for the cottage in Normandy, where they meet G., B., and their two daughters. G. and B. know all about their troubles, but they are discreet. At one point G. comments, referring to her companion, "He doesn't handle these situations very well."

And B. protects G.: "She doesn't like talking about stuff like that."

He does not insist. He broaches the subject only once, with B. They are alone in the car, and he asks, "Do you think we'll get past this?"

"I don't know," B. answers.

A reply that puts a knot in his stomach, because he has all the confidence in the world in B., who always approaches problems on a theoretical plane, with a detachment much like his own attitude to his characters. G. is like that too. She is also a writer. She talks about B., and protects and

loves him as she does the creatures she invents.
And similarly her companion, even though he
doesn't write.

Whenever he feels a need to unravel a complex
situation, he turns to G. and B. And he always
listens to what they have to say.

In the car that day, after B. said he didn't know
whether they would make it or not, he outlines the
latest developments of the crisis, emphasizing the
points that are favorable to him and passing
quickly over the others. Then he asks the question
again: "Do you think we'll get past this?"

"Probably," says B., who clearly is not fooled.

"Only probably?"

"I don't have all the facts."

"Yes you do. I've told you everything."

"In that case, yes. I think you stand a good
chance of getting past it."

They are silent for a moment, and then he
throws the slightly loaded dice again, more hon-
estly this time. "It'll take time. . . ."

"A lot," B. agrees.

"How much?"

They drive on in silence.

The cottage is nestled between two other cottages
of the same type, which similarly stand between

others of the same type, all of them forming a recreation center for upper-middle-class professionals of the same type.

Every morning all these professionals of the same type converge on the bakery to buy croissants of the same type. After which, with wife and progeny in tow, they head for a gigantic pool equipped with Jacuzzis, artificial waves, slides, aquatic bars, plastic trees, squalling children, and persistent chlorine. To get to the pool you have to walk through the activity center, a sort of mall where pizza, greasy fried chicken, and Chantilly desserts are on offer. Soft music plays in the background: Vivaldi's "Spring," Handel's *Water Music,* and, on good days, Bach's Third Brandenburg Concerto. The mall opened out onto the recreation area: Ping-Pong, tennis, squash, Pumping Pecs, Inc.

Horror at four thousand francs a week.

It's fun for the kids, she says.

He agrees.

Fortified by his excellent resolutions, he goes with her everywhere. He swims with the First Child, plays in the puddles with the Baby, and finally rediscovers his wife in their now common attitude toward you-know-what. This period reminds them of another, three years earlier, when they followed a couple they knew to a club in

Tunisia where the activities were not very different, though somewhat more varied: all the nice
people got drunk in groups, gorged themselves in
groups, and tried to rape women in groups.
Groups of the same type.

They went for a ride in a mule-drawn cart, and
since the idea of lounging in the backseat while a
poverty-stricken peasant held the reins up front
was repugnant to him, he insisted on sitting
alongside the driver, suggesting a wholly absurd
solidarity with the toiling classes.

A week after their arrival in Tunisia, they
caught the first plane out.

Though they have always agreed on the important
things, Normandy is not Tunisia. Although they
both scorn yuppies on bicycles as they had jerks in
cutaway bathing suits, they are no longer of one
mind, for they now part company on the important
things. They are both sad, but for discordant
reasons: she laments the other man's absence, while
he laments hers. He wishes she had the decency
not to show her grief in front of him, but he
understands why that's not possible. His heart is
touched by hers. For the first time he feels genuine
contempt for the other man. There are days when
he wants to stand up and ask him to think about

the effects of his deeds and words. For he will make him lose everything. Including his head.

She has not yet lost hers, but it is definitely elsewhere. His anger returns. He comes to feel that for her to express her pain so openly is like kissing the other man in front of him. You have no right to show your grief to someone else that way, unless that someone else is the cause of the grief. In which case you just walk away.

At night he avoids going to bed at the same time as she does. When he joins her she is asleep, her body padlocked by her hands, legs folded closed. He looks at her, brushes her skin. She moans and he goes back to the next room, thinking sadly to himself, If she can no longer spare me even a single gesture, I will leave her.

Yes, he will leave her. He would have to, for he could not live with a woman who would not give what she now refused him.

She has disarmed him, and now he must rearm himself.

"You are the person I love most in the world," she says.

———

Theirs, he thinks, is a tender love. Loves of passion always turn into tender loves—or into ashes. If he is the person she loves most in the world, then that makes him the fire's embers, and the warmth of the embers is deeper, denser, and more lasting than the vivacity of the flame.

"If I'm the person you love most in the world," he asks, "then how come your heart isn't in it when we make love?"

"You are the person I love most in the world," she replies, "but I don't feel like making love to you."

"Do you think that will last?"

"I don't know."

"I asked you the same question at the movies the other day, and you said we would again someday."

"Sometimes I think so, and sometimes I don't. Lots of couples live together without making love," she adds, artlessly.

"Not me," he says, definitively.

I shouldn't make love to her, he tells himself. I *must* not make love to her.

But he cannot help himself. Her body against his reassures him. If ever they can no longer hold each other, it will be over. But since she no longer opens her arms to him, he takes her.

"Why don't you get yourself a girlfriend?" she says.

Good shot, he says to himself. Thanks a lot.

If I want to keep her, he thinks, I have to stop making love to her. And if I can't make love to her, I'll have to make love to someone else.

Thus it is that he slowly begins to ease into a new reality, as she imposes one impossibility after another.

He now knows that the truce will not last. They have stopped playacting. On this day, the first of January, they consummate the breakup.

Happy New Year.

H E WAITED SEVEN DAYS AFTER
their return to Paris, and when nothing
changed in those seven days, he called a
friend, invited her to dinner, and spent a delicious
night with her.

He could have come home at three in the morning, but decided to return closer to eight. Just to
mark the parallel.

She asked no questions. None at all. It did not
matter to her what he did, and he felt better,
because of the delightful night.

He no longer wants to preserve their relationship
at any cost. She has eluded him so expertly, and
he has fought so hard in vain, that he now admits
to himself that other outcomes are possible. He
thinks it just might be that he has finally reached
the point she was at three months ago.

————

She telephones S. in front of him and talks—loudly—about one of their female friends who is now living alone after leaving her husband. "I ran into her just the other day," she says, "and she looks wonderful: beautiful, free, and happy. Ten years younger."

Bitch, he thinks.

"That's funny," he says when she hangs up. "I saw her yesterday, and I thought she looked fat and ugly—downright hideous, in fact."

Bastard, she thinks.

He and V. grant an interview to a journalist, who, it turns out, is accompanied by a photographer he knows. "I just saw your wife," she informs him, "walking down the street with some other guy. If I were you, I wouldn't be too happy."

He shuts down, and V. answers the questions for both of them. "Don't do anything stupid," V. says to him as they walk up the rue de l'Ancienne-Comédie after the interview.

He goes home and calls his wife. "Who was the man?" he asks.

"I don't know what you're talking about," she replies.

"Move out," he says. "Now."

That evening he is waiting for her in the living room when she comes home.

"Look," she says, "I told you it was over between me and the other man. Just because we still see each other . . ."

"Move out!" he repeats.

She nods. "Okay. Just give me a few days."

On her way to the door, she turns to him and adds, like a diabolical afterthought, "Except I'm taking my children with me."

He stands up.

"They're not *your* children. They're *our* children."

"Sure they are. But I'm taking them with me."

"Why?"

"Because I'm their mother."

"And I'm their father!" he shouts.

"That's not enough," she says with a pretty smile.

He is devastated.

———

He calls R. for help, and R. takes him to dinner. Later they spend three hours walking along the black waters of the Saint-Martin Canal in a blinding rain, each wearing his motorcycle helmet instead of carrying an umbrella. They do not look at the bridges, the boats, or the rusty wire fences. The pale glow of the street lamps guides their steps.

"I'm going to lose my children," he says.

"You won't."

"Yeah I will. She'll have them every day and I'll see them now and then."

"You'll see them in your own home, in better circumstances. The rapport will be different."

"I'll be a toy father."

"You'll always be their father."

"I've been putting the First Child to bed for five years, tucking him in, telling him stories. Now it's over. Over!"

He turns to R., who loves his daughter passionately and to whom he feels so close tonight, not only as a friend but also as a father, for R., too, is quite capable of sleeping at the foot of his daughter's bed. "Could you imagine living without your child?" he asks.

R. shakes his head.

"We love them just like the women do, but they can take them from us because we're men."

———

The next day, in the bathroom, he says to his wife, "If you take the First Child from me, I'll kill you."

Another day: "You humiliate my heart."

"You humiliate my body."

"How so?"

"Because it's humiliating for a woman to make love with a man she doesn't desire anymore."

"I've never humiliated anyone, and I'll never lay a hand on you again."

From then on he never spends a single night, a single day, a single hour in bed with her. All of a sudden he no longer wants her.

Since the idea had apparently not occurred to her, he asked her to stop walking around naked in front of him. He now went about methodically severing the branches of their ancient tree, one by one.

He cannot stand hearing people say that she is beautiful, or that she is sweet. He wants people to hate her. He doesn't love her anymore. The only thing that matters now is the structure that had been theirs, their family, and that structure, because of her, is now on a countdown to collapse.

On the eighty-seventh day she poured herself a whiskey and Perrier, sat down in an armchair, and said, "The other man and I are going to live together."

He did not budge. He thought that this was probably what she had been waiting for, the event that did not depend on him, the thing she had mentioned that day in Le Touquet. He was very calm.

"We're looking for an apartment."

"What about the children?"

"They'll come and live with us."

The "us" was hateful to him.

"Maybe you could work out some kind of transition for them."

"What do you mean?"

"Live alone for a while, so the break won't be so painful. Then you can move in with the other man."

"No. I've already spoken to the First Child. There's no problem."

He stared blankly at her, dazed.

"You already talked to him?!"

"That surprises you?"

"Yes it does. Very deeply."

He felt no anger. Just a huge discouragement. And something like disgust.

He stood up, went to the wooden plank he used as a desk in the apartment, took off his wedding ring, and dropped it on the makeshift table. Then he turned to her and asked, "What exactly did you say to the First Child?"

"That he was going to live with a new man and his daughter. He was very happy."

He thought she had lost her mind. That the other man had caused her to lose her mind.

For several days he tried to banish the images from his brain, but he couldn't manage it. The Baby growing up with a stranger. The First Child playing with the daughter. He knocking on *their door* to pick up his children. She greeting him, polite but cold, very much the woman comfortably settled in her new life, calling the children to come and say hello to their father. And their father, living alone, miserably contemplating this fine and well-built structure, taking his boys to McDonald's for supper and to the Luxembourg Gardens on rainy afternoons. The First Child would be awkwardly reassuring. The Baby would not understand who was this man his brother called Daddy. They would ask to go home to their mother's, where their toys were, where the little girl was, because that's where their *home* now was. Hey man!

My children will forget me, he thought.

They'll never forget you, S. and R. told him. You're their father.

I'm going to lose them, he cried. They're going to disappear from my life!

He went to see a lawyer. He picked a woman, thinking it would be easier for her if they divorced by mutual consent. He wanted no more warfare. He wanted a peace without open wounds. He wanted his children, reasonably.

"Is there any way I can get custody?" he asked.

"No," his counselor replied.

"Why not?"

"Because when the children are less than ten years old, judges always give custody to the mother. Unless she's a notorious prostitute."

"So I have no recourse at all?"

"Not quite."

There were a number of things he could do, one more vile than the next, and all very risky to boot. It was not his way, and not his wife's either. Not even for the children.

He decided to come to terms.

―――――

"I went to see a lawyer," he said to her that evening. "If you want, we can talk to her together. As far as the children are concerned, I'd like to suggest this arrangement: the Baby's legal residence would be with you, the First Child's with me. Both of us would have mutually agreed visitation rights, and we would share parental responsibility."

"Which means what?"

"We would both remain guardians of both children. Officially, one would live with you, the other with me. In reality, we would jointly decide where they would live and how frequent the visits would be."

She hesitated for a long time. Then: "Okay. On one condition: that they are never told the terms of this deal."

"Of course," he replied.

At first he had hoped to keep all three of them, then two, and finally one. Now only a half remained to him. But at least it was something. Fuck this society, he thought.

HE DOES NOT LOOK AT HER. HE will never look at her again. She is too beautiful. He cannot stand the severe expression that never seems to leave her face, and still less the occasional radiant smile and the clarity of her gaze, either of which would melt him if he so much as glanced at them, which is why he averts his glance when he talks to her, turns his head when he passes by her, goes to another room whenever she enters the one he is in. He knows that in all this he, too, is cultivating the pernicious weeds of breakup, and that he is doing it so thoroughly that they will never be able to turn back, to rediscover the meadows of their former loves. But he doesn't give a damn anymore. He has done his best, and now he cannot go on.

He spends his evenings out, hitting on women with every available tactic, promising trips he actually plans to make, even setting dates. He is staking out the ground he feels he needs, trying to construct upstream islands to replace the solid ground from which he had been ejected. In the end he gets hopelessly confused, mixing up names and personal histories, forgetting what he has said to one and not to another. But the women are wonderful, for they help him. Without asking anything in return. They are sensitive, tender, and generous, and he loves them, with or without the icing.

But he never sleeps anywhere else but home. He wants to be there for the children. When he comes in, often at dawn, he drags his wheeled cot into the First Child's room, picks up the pillow she has been kind enough to leave outside the door of what had been their bedroom, and falls into a whiskey-leadened sleep.

He feels an emptiness on his left hand where his wedding ring once was. From time to time his thumb drifts over to his ring finger and feels nothing there. When he washes his hands, he rubs bare skin. We were as quick to separate as to fall in love, he thinks.

He casts furtive glances at her hand. Even

after she takes the rings—his rings—from her left hand, the jewelry he bought her to celebrate the birth of each of the children will remain: three gold bands from Van Cleef & Arpels on her right hand, a Cartier watch on her left wrist.

It will hurt him terribly when she removes the aquamarine that marked their first meeting and the gold wedding band.

During the day he spends all his time with the children, both the First Child and the Baby.

"You never used to pay any attention to the Baby," she taunts him. "It wasn't until this crisis that you finally discovered him."

"Fatherhood is not measured by the economy of gestures," he replies.

He had chosen his son's name, he was his son's father, and he had always considered himself as such. And over and over and over again he thought, with horror, that at the age of eleven months that son would disappear from his life for many long years. He would not teach him to walk. Or to speak. He would not see him grow up. And he knew he would never be content with these meager crumbs.

———

The First Child is hurting. "I'm gonna do a divorzation," he says, where he means "demonstration." When his mother takes him to the doctor and the pediatrician asks him how he is, he says, "I'm fine . . . except for this divorzation shit." And one day he says to his father, "Daddy, if you're as smart as Robin Hood, how come you can't figure a way out?"

On Wednesday he clings to his father and cries when he leaves. When the father comes home from lunch one afternoon, he finds his son lying face down on his bed, dead pale and complaining that his tummy hurts.

A memory is triggered. Twenty-eight years ago, when his father left home, he went to bed and refused to see anyone for several hours, pretending that his stomach hurt. But it wasn't his stomach that hurt. He hurt all over.

He lies down beside his son and puts his arms around him. The night before, when the boy complained of a different ache, the mother said, "Don't take it seriously. He's just acting out because of the divorce." But he can't help it. His child is in pain, as he had been. So he comforts him. They comfort each other.

Late in the day the mother telephones. He is in a rage. "Get the hell out of here already!" he screams. "If you won't do it for me, at least do it for the boys. You've been feeding us this 'I don't know' poison for four months now. Enough!"

The mother hangs up without a word.

She's still here, he thinks to himself, furious. Comfortably ensconced in her apartment, waiting until she and the other man find a home in which she will live with the children she takes from me.

He goes back into his son's room. The First Child is still in bed. He doesn't breathe a word.

"Get up," the father says.

"Why, Daddy?"

"We're going out to buy toys."

The child says he cannot walk. His father dresses him, picks him up, and takes him to the toy store. He is not buying his son. He is buying toys for his son.

"We think we've found an apartment," the mother announces that evening.

She describes it: very large, light and beautiful, ridiculously expensive, near the park. They will move in as soon as possible. The children will be happy there.

Later she rolls the cot into the living room, next to the Baby's crib, which has been moved out.

"This way you can sleep in your bedroom," she says.

He refuses. "I'll stay with my son," he says.

One morning he hears the mother say to the First Child, "You have to be nice to Daddy. Otherwise he'll yell at me."

Another morning, when she scolds the child and he snaps that he will go and get his father, she says, "You're going to have to get used to seeing your daddy less often."

He is in the bathroom when he hears this. He smiles an evil smile and mutters, very softly, "Half the time."

When the First Child is hateful with his mother, he is secretly and confusingly content. But also ashamed. After she leaves for work on Wednesday, he hands the First Child the phone and says, "Call Mommy. Say something nice to her."

His friends disappear one after the other. Realizing that they can no longer help, they withdraw to await the denouement. He leaves them to their deathwatch. They're right, he thinks. There is a stench of death about us.

———

One evening he gets a phone call from E. and F., whom he has known for a long time. He tells them of the impending breakup, and they invite him to dinner. "Some other friends are coming too," F. tells him when he gets there.

The three of them spend about half an hour alone. For twenty minutes they chat about this and that, and then, only because the conversation has slowly drifted in that direction, E. says, "I don't want to pressure you to talk about the separation, but . . ." He then launches into an account of the crisis he and F. went through a few years before. At that point F. jumps in, and he watches, stupefied, as they exchange memories, politely batting back and forth a ball whose course he mutely follows.

The other invited guests arrive at nine. They sit down to eat, talk about this and that, have the last drink, and head home, each in his own direction. E. and F., intimate friends though they are, never ask so much as a single question about the change in his life.

I'm scaring people, he says to himself as he drives home.

———

He draws some consolation from picturing the new life he will lead after her departure. He will charm women, throw parties.

He does throw parties, and he manages to seduce a few women too. But he is unable to settle into this new life, because she is still a chattering, sadistic presence in it.

Sometimes, despite everything, a precarious calm settles between them. One day she accompanies him to a television interview—for him more than for herself. She knows how afraid he is whenever he's invited to a literary broadcast.

They go into the studio together, and she takes his arm. There is a tenderness between them, and he thinks to himself, If only it could be like this afterward!

"I don't like it when you talk so violently," she says when they get home. "You're much more intelligent than the words you spew out when you're angry. I like you better the way I know you are."

He doesn't answer. She wants it all. To leave and for him to calmly watch, ingratiating smile in place, as she destroys everything he holds dearest.

He disengages his arm from hers.

———

His mother called. He could no longer postpone telling her about the breakup, so he confessed everything.

"You covered up pretty well," was her first comment. Then she asked how the children were holding up. She displayed admirable discretion, as always. But she did loose one barb: "I don't see why she wanted the Baby. I mean, a crisis like this, that brings everything down in four months, you'd think she would have seen it coming."

Later they will talk about the past.

He will then realize that the special rapport he has nurtured with the First Child may have been partly the product of his own history, of his desire to create with his son the bonds he had failed to establish with his own father, despite every effort. The first of those efforts, a considerable one indeed, came when he was ten: his decision, on his own and without the slightest outside influence, to go and live with his father, the jilted one, whose pain had moved him.

In his adult memories he could find nothing beyond that pain—no tenderness, no intimacy— that might have justified a decision of such great import. Before he opted to go and live with him, his father was no more than a hand leaving the red traces of paternal iron on his butt. Which was probably another reason why he had never been strict with his own children: he did not want to be like his father, and he had always rebelled against that kind of authority, which seemed cruel and unfair to him. He didn't want to repeat *that*.

He will also come to realize that if he found it so easy to imagine living alone with the First Child, which would mean separating him from his brother, it was because he wanted to repeat with his son what he himself had done, believing that separating his children from each other would not hurt them any more than his being separated from his own brother and sister had hurt him. And once he understands that, he will let go, for he has never considered himself an example worth emulating.

His mother did not chide him for having waited so long to tell her what was going on, filling her in just a few frames before the denouement. Had she done so, he would not have tried to defend himself. But he was well aware of the reason for his reticence. In his parents' divorce, his father had suffered just as he was suffering now. His mother had walked out. Just like his wife. He saw each of them in the other, and he blamed each for what he confusedly resented in the other. That being the case, silence was the best policy.

His mother's voice contained all the tenderness, love, and commiseration he needed. But he couldn't bear listening to it. He could never stand it when his mother treated him like a child, and he had an explanation for that too. He had once thought of it this way: If I chose to go with my father, it was because my mother didn't love me. I sensed it at the time, and later on I was told it.

Yes, he was told it.

But now he imagined what might be a new reason, one buried in the limbo of guilt. And of childhood.

He is ten years old, and his father has moved out. He, his brother, and his sister are about to leave for winter vacation. (He would always hate winter sports.) In the hallway of their big house he runs into his mother, who has just bought parkas, ski pants, and shoes for the children. They are alone. "This way you'll be all set when you decide to live with me," she says.

He looks at her. And he answers, "I don't want to live with you, Mommy. I want to go with Daddy."

He does not remember a word of what happened next. It's like a black hole. He must have been intent on wiping it from his memory at all costs. But it is possible, even probable, that he had heard in his mother's voice the love and tenderness that he had never been able to tolerate since then. It is as if he had done all he could to erase every trace of the immeasurable sorrow she may have felt, the sorrow that he, little ten-year-old executioner, must surely have caused.

And that was why he had told his wife from the very beginning: We will never ask the children to choose, we will never burden them with so terrible a responsibility.

In this he was seeking to spare her and himself the pain that one or the other of their children would have inflicted. And to spare one or the other of their children any future pain born of this present one, for which they alone were responsible. Yes, for which they alone were responsible. It was as if, caught between hammer and anvil, he had realized that today's hammer threatened to become his sons' anvil. And it was to avoid that, to avoid poisoning his sons' memories, that on the evening of the ninety-fifth day he would lay down his arms and let his children leave.

O N T H E E I G H T Y - N I N T H D A Y H E
asked her when she and the other man
intended to move in together. She told
him that a problem had arisen. They had had to
postpone things for a few days, but nothing in the
basic decision had changed. She was still moving
out.

He knew she was moving out, but she would
move out alone.

She spent the ninetieth and ninety-first days
gloomily moping around the apartment. On the
ninety-second day she announced, "I'm going
alone. The other man isn't coming. It's definitely
over between us."

He was as still as marble. "Have you talked to
the First Child?" he asked.

She said she had. He did not ask what she'd

said. She was sad, and so was he. For her. But he was happy for his children.

On the ninety-third day he found these words written on the bathroom mirror in red lipstick, in capital letters:

MY DREAM IS TO FIND
AN APARTMENT AND MOVE OUT.

It occurred to him that morning that she might be paying him back for whatever wrong the other man had done her. It's going to be hell if she doesn't feel any guilt anymore, he said to himself.

By the evening of the ninety-fifth day hell was well and truly under way. She came home later than usual, wearing a black suit. No earrings. She stood in the living room and coldly declared, "I went to see a child psychologist and a lawyer."

She named the lawyer: an old girlfriend she had been politically active with in the mid-seventies.

"I'm taking both children with me," she said. "The law is on my side."

He was stunned.

"You can see them every Wednesday and every

other weekend. And possibly for an hour after school."

"You expect me to be a babysitter for my children?" he asked.

"The law is on my side," she repeated.

"I didn't bring children into the world to be satisfied with these crumbs," he said.

She continued her exposition: "I'll file for divorce as soon as I move out. Otherwise you could hit me with a desertion suit."

"I wouldn't do anything like that," he replied. "How can you think I would stoop so low?"

"I don't know what you're capable of when you're angry."

"Yeah, but now I know what you're capable of!"

For the first time they discussed the modalities of the divorce. He told her that if they had to resort to the courts to adjudicate the termination of their love, he would despise her forever, her and their whole relationship. And he would never see her again. "That's the responsibility you'll bear before your children," he added.

He walked out, slammed the door, and went to see his fourth-floor neighbor. He came back at dawn, dead drunk.

———

It's just a flare-up, his friends say. She'll never do anything like that.

He knows that. But he also knows he has lost his children. For he will never take any legal steps to get them back. You don't get your children back. You either keep them or lose them. That's how he sees it. And I'm losing them. Which is why he fell apart.

He cannot look at his sons anymore. He does not know how to talk to them. He wants to love them less, so greatly does he fear the hopelessness of the terrible moment of departure.

He repeats that he is keeping the apartment. It is his children's apartment, and when they come to visit, they will recognize the place where they grew up and the man who raised them. He wants to keep the house so as not to lose his sons entirely. And so that they can come together again in this place that has been and would remain their own.

He clings to this prospect as the last lifeline of his ruined family life.

———

We are reproducing our parents' schemas so perfectly, he tells her. Me alone and cut off, you alone with the children.

He meets V. in Reims, where the city council holds an affair in their honor. After the toasts, the broadcasts, and the champagne lunch, he and V. sit in a literary café, drinking Bordeaux and being interviewed by two journalists. At a certain point he puts his hand in his pocket and realizes the box of Valium is gone. He panics. He surreptitiously feels around under the table with his foot as he answers the journalists' questions. Nothing. He looks around. He notices a man near the counter staring at an object cupped in the folded palm of his hand. The man raises his head and glances around. Their eyes meet. The man opens his hand. "It's mine!" he shouts.

The man walks over and hands him the box of Valium. He introduces himself: W., manager of the café. His smile is tinged with sarcasm.

"Why are you staring at me like that?"

"No reason."

"You can't know what's in that box. There's no label and . . ."

W. does not reply. He keeps smiling.

"You've taken them too?"

"Yes."

W. walks away. That evening, D.R., one of the great contemporary photographers, invites the two of them to dinner at the best restaurant in town. W. sits down beside him, drapes his arm over his shoulders, and asks, "What's wrong?"

He, too, is a full-fledged brother of the Knights of Valium.

These evenings out do not stop him from thinking, but at least they allow him to think at some distance, which is better than haunting the site of his discomfiture. When he goes home, he finds hell still raging on.

She has, in fact, lost all sense of guilt and is now constantly on the attack. "It's not that I'm leaving," she says. "It's that we're breaking up."

Before she was through she would forget everything that had happened and would reverse the roles.

"Don't ever forget the origin of this split," he replies.

She blames him for everything and anything, lashing out all the more, he believes, because she has been unable to play out her affair with the other man. But he admires her when, immediately after hurling some clever and painful barb, she suddenly draws back and acts softer and almost caring, as though she has pulled herself up short and said, Wait a minute, don't go too far!

Night after night she keeps him informed of her search for an apartment. Day after day she keeps saying, "My dream is to move out."

"So get the hell out!" he answers.

One morning, in a rage, he grabs her by the arm and pushes her onto the bed. "No violence!" she shouts. "No physical violence!"

As though he were a satyr and she a feminist zealot ready to defend herself.

But he has never beaten her. He shakes her a little to make her shut up, just to make her shut up. Let her move out already, let her stop hectoring him! After four months he's had it for good.

Sometimes, when they bicker, the First Child comes into the room brandishing a plastic sword. "I'm the argument chief! I'm in charge!"

They fall silent. Sometimes he laughs.

She now sleeps in the living room with the Baby, assigning herself the most temporary place in the apartment.

He moves back into their former bedroom, no longer wanting to sleep beside the First Child, with whom he will not be living. Nor does he want to wake up beside him with the thought that these are their last nights together.

She telephones to ask him to sign as the guarantor of the apartment she has found. He refuses.

"You won't loan me any money either?"

"No!"

She hangs up on him.

He cannot help her move into a place where his children will live without him. He tries, but he simply can't.

He feels guilty. He wonders whether he ought to be the one to move out, since he is not keeping the children. But it is a decision he cannot make. He clings desperately to the only trench she has not yet taken.

He goes out, drinks, smokes, snorts lines, smokes joints, screws. But every morning, inexorably, he comes back to his children's home. And when he sees their mother curled up under the covers in the darkness of the living room, he sometimes feels like lying down beside her, silent and motionless, and taking her in his arms. My poor love, my poor love, I told you no one would love you as much as I do.

At moments like this he asks himself how they came to this, and he gnashes his teeth at the monstrous waste. But it's too late. They've gone too far. The battle is done, and it is as an unarmed sentinel that he goes to his own bed, there to collapse for a little while until he is awakened by the cries of his children.

He finds a statuette she had given him a few years before: a witch holding aloft the severed head of the man she loved. He had hated this gift at the time, and he hates it still. She is not a witch, he says to himself, and I still have my head.

When they are together in the apartment and he listens to her or looks at her, things he had never liked about her but had thought he could get used to now seem odious and intolerable. "I've gotten to where you were four months ago," he tells her.

And he understands her.

———

One day, sick and tired of waiting for her to move out, he calls half the real estate agencies in Paris. It takes him three hours to find an apartment about two hundred yards from his own.

He calls her and suggests that they take a look at it that afternoon. She agrees. That evening she goes to see it alone. She likes it, and the next day he offers to sign as her guarantor. Three days later the agency informs them that he has been accepted. They have forty-eight hours to sign the lease.

That night he came home at dawn. She was giving the Baby his bottle and did not hear him come in. He looked at them through the glass partition of the living room and felt a pang in his heart. He went to the bedroom, tore off the top sheet of a pad, sat down on the bed, and scribbled the final missive of their relationship. In it he asked her if they could wipe the slate clean and start from scratch.

She gave him her answer the next day. It was no.

Unbeknownst to her, he spent the next forty-eight hours looking for another apartment. For himself.

He had decided that this one was no more than the empty shell of a ruined structure. He wanted a place that would charm the children, something with a terrace, for example, where he could set up a sandbox and a swing. He did not want to get ahead of himself, so he told her nothing. But he knew his own mind.

The evening before the deadline for signing the lease on the new apartment, she spoke the words he had been waiting for: "Why don't you take it instead?"

He laughed. "Because it's not up to me to move out."

"It's not up to the children either."

"If you had moved in with the other man, the question of the apartment never would have arisen. I would have kept it."

"But that's not the way it worked out."

He spent the night out. It seemed to him that although he had good reasons for wanting to stay, they were weightless compared to the interests of the children. He pictured them living in a smaller place, having to get up a bit earlier to get to school every morning, having to change their space and their habits. He couldn't live with it.

"Cancel the appointment this evening," he said when he got home. "I'll move out."

———

He did not take the nearby apartment, because he now wanted to make a clean break. Change neighborhoods, change lives, forget. Start over.

"I'm very proud of you for deciding to move out," R. told him.

But all he felt was disarray.

WE COULD KEEP A CAR IN COM-
mon, he suggested.

You could do your laundry here,
she said.

Tell me how much money you need, he said.

Keep the key to the house, she said.

And: Come for dinner whenever you want.

They were trying to shape their future relations, both seeking to be generous and magnanimous. They were afraid of what was to come.

They said these things as they divided up the books. The First Child helped. They had presented his father's move to him as a game.

When the shelves were demolished, emptied of a quarter of their volumes, he sat down in front of the boxes. He was sad, and so was she.

Alone for the first evening in the home that would now be his, sitting on the carpet and watching the falling snow, sitting in total silence, in turbid immobility, he was suddenly seized by panic at the thought of having to spend all his time in this space where he would no longer hear his children's voices.

He went outside, jumped on his motorcycle, and sped to his family's home. He kissed his sons, then left again.

When he got back he remembered the words of K., his screenwriter friend: "You'll be tossed out, you'll be without a home, without your children. . . ."

Four and a half months after the outbreak of the crisis, she had thrown him out of her life, out of his home, out of his neighborhood, out of his garret, and far from his children. The war had been lost.

H E STOPS TAKING VALIUM. OR almost.

He sees his children twice a week. He is learning to live without them, as they are learning to live without him.

A part of himself has been severed, and he feels an empty space in his body and in his world. It is like trying to touch a missing limb, a thing that no longer exists.

He is an ephemeral presence for his children, and they are too weighty an absence.

He cannot stand to watch family commercials on television. He crosses the street when he passes a school or a toy store. He avoids parks on Wednesdays and Saturdays, averts his eyes when friends talk about their kids. He detests words like vacation, child care, snack, recreation, teacher, babysitter. He cannot watch children playing in the street. When he happens to notice an object belonging to one of his sons, he feels a quick, sharp pain like the prick of a needle. His eyes suddenly fill with tears—and dry as quickly. When he goes near the photographs of them pinned to the walls of his office, he feels anger and pain, loss and waste, a kind of death. My children have been stolen from me, he thinks.

The First Child is very cruel to him. "I'm bad because you're not there anymore," he says. "How come you divorced? How come you threw me in the garbage?"

He doesn't answer. At moments like this he feels horror at his wife, who has inflicted this injustice which he now has to bear in silence. He lost the war, as honorably as possible, but he is seen as the one responsible because he was the one who moved out.

When he goes to her place, he always kisses her when he arrives but never when he leaves. He hates her for having taken his boys from him, for having amputated a part of his past.

He sits in a chair in the living room that had so long been his and in which he is now a visitor. When he takes the Baby in his arms he does not know how to hold him. He gropes for bits and pieces of a new language. When he leaves, his child cries. He thinks, and he writes: If it were possible, I would keep both my boys, I would move again and live with them.

I'll never have any more children, he says.

He closes his eyes, his ears, and his mouth to his former life.

But when he weakens, she alone can soothe him. Because she is the mother and he is still the father. "At school they asked the First Child to draw a house," she tells him one day. "He drew two. Daddy's and Mommy's. They were identical."

One evening, a few weeks after the separation, the First Child telephoned one of his friends and said, very nonchalant, "I'm at my father's. We got divorced."

He believed that the children had been shielded from trauma. He was very proud of that. Proud of himself and proud of his wife.

The day would come when he would feel better and she worse. The day would come when it would be her turn to find that anger and blame were ways of facilitating breakups. Then she would defend herself before third parties from blows he had not dealt her, blackening him to whitewash herself. It would sadden him immensely to know she was so lost. The day would come when he would want her to be happy, and soon—as soon as possible. The day would come when she would walk him to his car with the children, and he would leave them to a lugubrious Saturday, while he set out for Trouville. And throughout the entire trip, between the road and his memory, he would see in his mind's eye the silhouette of this woman he had loved so deeply walking down the sidewalk with their two children, and he would realize that whatever happened, whether life was hard or evil, protracted or easy, these three would forever be his.

And he would tell himself: Let our story, sealed now in our dreams and recollections, remain there as a delicate vestige of elegance.

ON THE THIRTY-FIRST DAY AFTER he moved out, he was awakened at three in the morning by a phone call from C., the daughter of J., the woman he had lived with for ten years, long ago. C. was in tears. "My brother killed himself," she said.

H. had jumped off the roof of the tallest building in Jussieu.

He loved H., who was twenty years old.

He went with M. and A. to the morgue to identify the body. Then he called his wife to tell her what had happened.

They saw each other at the church on the morning of the burial. His brother was there as well. His brother had always been there at the terrible moments of his life. His sister too, in another way.

The three of them sat on a pew a little off to the side. His wife wore dark glasses. They listened to the Chaconne of Bach's Second Partita for Violin, which he had chosen for H. When the sermon started he left, because he couldn't stand the homilies. When it was over he came back. He went to the coffin, embraced A., his old companion, and her daughter. They held each other for a long time, fighting despair, and then he disentangled himself and fled to a far corner of the church. His wife found him there. She put her arms around him and said, "Courage, baby . . ."

Paris, October 1990–April 1991

A NOTE ABOUT THE TRANSLATOR

Jon Rothschild's translation of Alain Peyrefitte's *The Immobile Empire* received wide acclaim. He lives in New York, where he recently completed work on a translation of a biography of Georges Simenon.